Holly Webb
Illustrated by Sophy Williams

Contents

STRIPES PUBLISHING LIMITED
An imprint of the Little Tiger Group
1 Coda Studios, 189 Munster Road,
London SW6 6AW

Imported into the EEA by Penguin Random House Ireland,
Morrison Chambers, 32 Nassau Street, Dublin D02 YH68

A paperback original
First published in Great Britain in 2020

ISBN: 978-1-78895-199-9

A CIP catalogue record for this book is available from the British Library.

Printed and bound in the UK.

MIX
Paper from
responsible sources
FSC® C020471
www.fsc.org

The Forest Stewardship Council® (FSC®) is a global, not-for-profit
organization dedicated to the promotion of responsible forest management
worldwide. FSC defines standards based on agreed principles for
responsible forest stewardship that are supported by environmental, social,
and economic stakeholders. To learn more, visit www.fsc.org

10 9 8 7 6 5 4 3 2

Sammy the Shy Kitten

For Daisy

Chapter One

"See you later, Mum!" Emma waved as her mum drove off down the bumpy lane that led to Ivy Bank Stables. She was looking forward to seeing her best friend Keira, but she would see most of her riding-class friends at school on Monday. Really she wanted to say hello to the ponies and the cats that lived at the stables too.

Emma didn't always see the cats –
they were all very shy, almost wild.
She wasn't even sure how many of
them there were, no one was. Liz,
who owned the riding school, said she
thought there were five. But Emma
was almost certain there were six, and
that the skinny ginger cat was actually
two skinny ginger cats. Once she
thought she'd seen him strolling along
the roof of the feed store only seconds
after he'd been sunbathing out by the
paddock.

Liz put down food and water for the
cats, but only once a day. Mostly they
lived by hunting. They earned their
keep by getting rid of the mice and rats
that sniffed around the stables after the
horses' feed.

"Hello, Sparky," Emma murmured, going to pat the nose of the grey she usually rode in her class. The pony snorted and put his nose over the half-door of his stall. He nudged happily at her hand, searching for an apple or a carrot. He knew Emma always brought him treats. Emma giggled and brought out a piece of carrot. "And I've got Polos for afterwards, if you're good," she whispered. "But don't tell the others. I'll just go and let Liz know I'm here, then I'll be back to tack you up."

Emma looked around hopefully for the cats as she went over to find Liz, but none of them seemed to be around. She crouched down and peeped behind the tulips in the little flowerbed in front of the office. The ginger cat (one of the ginger cats, anyway) practically lived in the flowerbed, and sometimes he'd let her stroke him. Sure enough, there he was, curled up tightly into a stripey ball. He opened one yellow-green eye and glared at her. He obviously didn't want to be petted.

Emma sighed and put her head round the office door.

"Hi, Liz. Mum dropped me off a bit early so I could say hello to the ponies. I wanted to see if I could stroke Tiggy too, but I can't find her."

Tiggy was Emma's favourite of the stable cats – she was black and had longer fur than the others, with a thick bushy tail. She spent a lot of time lying in the sun and grooming, cleaning bits of hay out of her pretty fur.

Liz had looked up, smiling, when she first spotted Emma, but now her smile faded. "I haven't actually seen her for a couple of days. I'm starting to get a bit worried. I know the cats aren't really pets and they wander around all over the place, but usually Tiggy's the friendliest of them all. She doesn't disappear like Susie and Ginger, and she's almost always in the yard."

Emma nodded, frowning. "I don't think I've ever been to the stables and not seen her."

"She's been so hungry lately, but she hasn't come to the food bowls," Liz sighed. "I'm sure I'd have noticed her."

Emma glanced out at the bowls. Liz kept them by the bench in the yard, which had a wooden canopy built over it. It meant that the food stayed dry and the nervous cats didn't have to go inside for it. Emma smiled as she saw Susie, a thin little tabby, slinking over to see if there was anything left. But then she turned back towards Liz.

"So … Tiggy hasn't eaten anything for two days?" she asked anxiously.

Liz shook her head. "Not from here, I don't think. She's a good mouser, so maybe she's just been hunting more. I wish I'd seen her around, though."

Emma nibbled her bottom lip. "At least the stables is quite far from the main road," she said slowly. Her Auntie Grace's cat, Whisky, had been hit by a car a couple of years ago and had broken his leg really badly. He was better now, but Auntie Grace hated him going round the front of the house. She always tried to tempt him back inside if she saw him sitting on the front wall.

Liz smiled at her. "Exactly. I'm probably worrying over nothing."

She didn't make Emma feel much better, though. Where could Tiggy have gone?

"Anyway," Liz said briskly. "We should get on. The others will be here by now." She got up and put an arm round Emma's shoulders. "Don't worry. You know what cats are like – especially these half-wild ones. We'll get all upset and then she'll stroll in without a care in the world." Emma giggled. But she wished that Tiggy would stroll in *now*.

Maybe it was because she was thinking about Tiggy, or maybe it was just a bad day, but nothing seemed to go right for Emma that morning. Tacking up Sparky took ages. He wouldn't stay still – he jittered and sidestepped and nibbled at her jacket. Then he nearly trod on her foot as she led him over to the outdoor arena.

"Are you OK?" her friend Keira asked, as she finally managed to get to the gate. "You look a bit stressed."

"Sparky's just being … Sparky," Emma sighed. "He's lovely when he wants to be but…"

Keira grinned and nodded. "I know. Maybe he's just excited."

"He's always excited!"

"Are you ready, girls?" Liz came over to check that their girths were tight. "Now, the jumps are a bit higher than last week, but you're all perfectly capable of clearing these fences. Just don't let the ponies try to take them too fast."

Emma nodded a little nervously. She really did love Sparky. The gentler ponies, like Keira's mount Jasmine, just didn't have as much personality as the bouncy grey. But she had a feeling that trying to keep Sparky calm and collected wouldn't be that easy today. Luckily they were going first so Sparky wouldn't get bored. The thrill of riding a fast, eager pony took over as they set off, and Emma had a huge smile on her face by the time they'd cleared the second jump.

Then somehow everything went wrong. Perhaps Sparky decided he didn't like the look of the new rainbow-striped rails that Liz had used for the third jump. He slid round to the left of the jump instead of going over. Emma did her best to encourage him on, but Sparky was determined – he swerved sideways round the jump, and Emma felt herself slipping out of the saddle. There was a horrible, slow moment when she knew she was falling. Then all of a sudden she was on the ground, with her ankle twisted and aching, and Sparky standing over her. He looked quite apologetic.

"Emma!" Liz came hurrying over, catching Sparky's reins and handing them to Keira. "Hold on to him, Keira, while I check Emma's all right."

"I don't think I rode him at it straight enough," Emma said, wincing as she tried to stand. "Ow, my ankle…"

Liz gently felt the ankle through Emma's boot. "I don't think it's swelling up. Do you want me to call Alex and get him to bring you an ice pack?"

"It's OK. Sorry I messed up…"

"No, you were doing really well. It looked like Sparky just decided against that jump. Can you put any weight on your ankle?"

"I think so." Emma blinked, trying not to cry.

Liz helped her up. "Are you sure you're all right?"

Emma nodded. "It was just a bit of a shock…"

"Look, sit down on the bench. We'll tie Sparky up to the fence, and I'll come and check on you again in a bit."

Liz went back to schooling the others over the jumps and Emma watched from the side of the arena, gently rubbing her ankle. It was starting to feel a bit better already. She clapped as Keira jumped Jasmine clear and her friend waved at her.

Emma stood up and leaned on the fence, testing the weight on her ankle. It was definitely feeling better. She was just thinking about asking Liz if it was OK to untie Sparky again, when she heard a strange squeaky noise behind her. She glanced round. The outdoor arena was next to a shabby old barn that Liz was planning to get rid of, so they could make the arena bigger. It was divided up into stalls for horses, but they weren't used any more. The noise was definitely coming from in there, though. Emma limped curiously over to the door – that was falling apart too, a couple of the boards had rotted away at the bottom.

She lifted the latch, pushed open the door and looked round it cautiously. Maybe a bird had got trapped inside – she didn't like the idea of it flapping out at her. But there was no bird, only the raspy creak of the door – and then that tiny, breathy little squeak again. Emma walked in slowly, following the noise. It sounded like it was coming from the stall at the end.

Emma stopped and peered round the open half-door. There was still some straw on the floor, piled up in the corner. The squeaking was coming from over there, and for one horrible moment Emma wondered if it was a rat.

Then a dark head looked up over the straw and Emma laughed in surprise.

"Tiggy!" she said, keeping her voice low. "Liz is really worried about you, you know. What are you doing in here?"

Tiggy eyed her cautiously, her ears flickering, and Emma frowned. She'd never heard Tiggy squeak like that before, she realized. And there was something else in the straw – something small and wriggly and dark. Actually there were several somethings…

"Oh! Tiggy, have you…?" Emma stepped closer, trying to lean over the door just a little so she could see without scaring the cat. She'd completely forgotten about her twisted ankle now. "You have! You've had kittens!"

Chapter Two

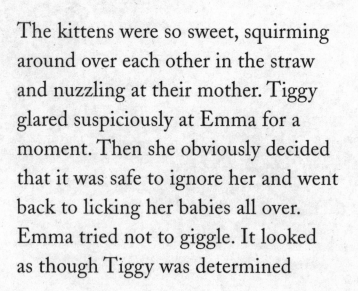

The kittens were so sweet, squirming around over each other in the straw and nuzzling at their mother. Tiggy glared suspiciously at Emma for a moment. Then she obviously decided that it was safe to ignore her and went back to licking her babies all over. Emma tried not to giggle. It looked as though Tiggy was determined that they would be just as beautifully groomed as she was.

"So that's why you were really hungry. It's OK, Tiggy. I won't come any closer." Emma hung on to the door post, counting. "It's three, isn't it?" she whispered. "Two black kittens and one grey tabby. I ought to go and tell the others…" But she didn't want to leave just yet. The kittens were so little Emma wondered when they'd been born.

"I'd better go and tell Liz," she said at last, slowly backing away. "Don't go anywhere, will you…" She had read about mother cats picking up their kittens in their mouths to move them if she thought they weren't safe. She hoped she hadn't scared Tiggy into doing anything like that. But Tiggy didn't look too worried. "I'll get Liz to find you some food too," Emma added, her eyes widening. "Oh, Tiggy, you must be starving!"

As soon as she was out of sight of Tiggy, Emma whisked round and limped out of the barn as fast as she could.

Liz waved when she saw her and hurried over. "Emma! I just noticed that you'd disappeared. How's your ankle? It doesn't look like it's swollen."

Emma shook her head, grinning at Liz. "No, it feels nearly better now. And I've found Tiggy."

"Oh, that's brilliant! Where was she? Is she all right?"

Emma giggled. "She's more than all

right. You have to come and see!"

"I need to watch the others. Can you show me at the end?" Liz glanced between Emma and the rest of the class, and Emma realized that of course she couldn't leave them riding without an instructor.

"It's OK. I don't think Tiggy's going anywhere." Emma folded her arms and glanced back at the barn.

Liz sighed. "I hope this is worth all the suspense, Emma! Come on, you'd better catch up with the others. Sparky looks very sorry for himself."

Sparky did seem to think that he'd been missing out. He brightened up as he saw Emma and jumped two clear rounds with her as soon as he was allowed back into the ring.

"You monster!" Emma told him affectionately, as she patted his nose afterwards. "You can have a Polo – here. But I don't think you deserve it. Why didn't you do that first time round, instead of tipping me off?" Sparky whiffled up the Polo from her hand eagerly and Emma smiled.

"I suppose if I hadn't fallen, I wouldn't have found the kittens. Oh, look, Liz is waving. It's the end of the lesson now – I can't wait for her to see them." She hugged Sparky round the neck and started to walk him back to the gate where the others were waiting. "I'm not showing you, though. I wouldn't trust you not to put your massive great clumpy feet on those kittens."

"What are you so excited about?" Keira asked, as she led Jasmine over towards Emma and Sparky.

"I found Tiggy! Liz hadn't seen her for a couple of days – she was getting worried. You have to come and see!"

Keira looked at her doubtfully. "Sorry, Emma. You know I'm scared of cats."

"I forgot! Sorry, I was just so excited." She bit her lip, not wanting Keira to miss out on the secret. But she knew her friend was especially frightened of the half-wild cats at the stables. "Come here." She leaned over to whisper in Keira's ear. "Tiggy's had kittens. In the old barn! Don't tell Liz yet, OK?"

Keira smiled. "Now I get why you're so excited. Are they cute?" She sounded a little bit wistful, as though she wished she wasn't so nervous around cats.

"I only saw them from a distance, but they were gorgeous. Are you sure you don't want just a little look?"

Keira shook her head. "Tiggy's so jumpy…"

Liz came up behind them. "Are you going to show me this big secret now?"

Emma nodded eagerly and Keira laughed. "She can't wait – I'm surprised she hasn't told everybody already! Here, I'll lead Sparky back."

Emma handed over the reins and hurried Liz along to the barn door. "Be really quiet!" she whispered, putting a finger up to her lips. Then she led the way inside, tiptoeing over the dusty floor.

"Where is she?" Liz hissed, and then she gasped as Emma pulled her sleeve and pointed into the stall. "Kittens! Oh, wow, I never even thought of that!"

"Three of them," Emma said, beaming. "Aren't they beautiful? Can we put down some food for Tiggy in here? I bet she's really hungry."

Liz nodded. "Yes, definitely. I'll go and get her some now. Gosh, three more cats. That's a lot…"

Emma looked up at her worriedly. "I hadn't thought about that."

Liz made a face. "Well, they are lovely, but I'm not sure how many more cats we can look after, to be honest. We've already got five. I suppose I should have expected this to happen, but none of them have had kittens till now. Probably we should have got them neutered, but they're all so shy. It was a nightmare the one time I had to take Susie to the vet because she'd been in a fight. She was really tricky to catch and she hated being in the car."

"So..." Emma swallowed – her mouth had gone dry with excitement. When she spoke again, her voice sounded oddly squeaky. "If the kittens couldn't stay here, would you want to find homes for them?"

Liz nodded slowly. "That would be perfect, wouldn't it? Nice homes where they'd be properly looked after."

Emma gazed thoughtfully at the wriggling bundles of fur. "I didn't think of them being pets," she murmured. "I thought they'd be a bit wild, like Tiggy."

Liz shook her head. "I think it's to do with how much they get used to people when they're little. Tiggy and Susie and the others are half-wild because they've never had a proper indoor home or spent much time around people. But it doesn't mean it has to be the same with these little ones."

Emma nodded. That made sense.

"How are you going to find them homes?" she said. "Would you just … ask people if they wanted them?"

Liz smiled at Emma. "I suppose so. Are you thinking you'd like a kitten? What would your mum and dad say?"

"I don't know." Emma sighed. "But I can ask. I love the idea of taming a little wild kitten!"

Liz snorted. "I wouldn't put it that way to your mum, Emma. She'd worry about you getting your fingers bitten off. Come on, let's go and find Tiggy something to eat."

Chapter Three

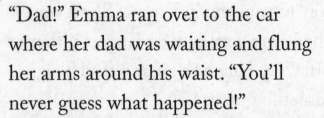

"Dad!" Emma ran over to the car where her dad was waiting and flung her arms around his waist. "You'll never guess what happened!"

Her dad blinked at her in surprise. "Did Sparky behave himself for once?"

Emma shook her head and laughed. "Nope, actually he was really tricksy and I fell off. But I'm OK! It's Tiggy

– she's had three kittens and I found them!"

"That's exciting! Are they really small?"

"I think they're only a day or two old," Emma explained. "Liz said Tiggy had disappeared for a couple of days, so I guess she went off to hide and make herself a little nest. The kittens are teensy – only about this big." She held her hands apart to show him. "Do you want to come and see?"

Dad wrinkled his nose. "I'd love to – but what about Tiggy? Isn't she really shy? If loads of people start tramping past her kittens, she might get upset."

Emma nodded. "I know. But Liz said that seeing as I found them, I can take some food back for Tiggy. You could come with me. Liz has made her a special treat – she found a bit of fish in the freezer. She reckons Tiggy deserves it!"

Dad grinned. "I haven't seen any tiny kittens for years – not since my cat Bella had kittens when I was about your age."

"Did she?" Emma looked surprised. "Didn't you have her neutered, then?"

"She was a stray that Granny May

adopted," Dad explained. "Well, she adopted us, really. She was sitting on the front doorstep one day when we came home from school. We hadn't even got as far as taking her to the vet, to be honest. We were just getting used to having a cat when the kittens arrived. We had her neutered after that… One litter of kittens was fun, but your gran didn't want to find homes for any more."

"You're so lucky," Emma sighed. "I wish we had kittens. Or a grown-up cat – I wouldn't mind." She gave her dad a sideways look. "Dad, if you really like cats, why don't we have one?"

Her dad looked thoughtful. "Well, it would have been tricky when me and Mum were both working full-time.

But I suppose now we've changed our shifts around we could…" Emma's parents both worked at the local hospital. "I don't know what your mum would think, though, Ems. She's never had a cat."

"I don't see how anybody could not like a tiny little kitten," Emma said coaxingly.

"Perhaps because it'll turn into a great big cat clawing the sofa? You know your mum likes everything really tidy in the house."

"A cat could be tidy…" Emma said hopefully. "Oh, Liz has got the food, look!" Liz was standing by the car-park gate, holding a couple of bowls. Emma grabbed her dad's arm, hauling him after her.

"We'll be really careful," she told
Liz, as she took the food bowl. "Oh,
you've got some water too. I was going
to ask you about that."

Emma's dad took the water bowl
and followed her across the yard to
the old barn. "I can hear them rustling
about," he whispered to Emma, as they
tiptoed over to the stall.

Tiggy was looking anxious, and
she half stood up as Emma and her

41

dad came to the door of the stall. The kittens squeaked a little and shifted around in the straw nest as their mother moved. Emma ducked her head, trying to see the kittens without staring at Tiggy – she knew from a cat programme she'd seen on TV that cats didn't like to make eye contact sometimes. "It's OK," she whispered. "We brought you some delicious food. Fish – can you smell it?"

She was sure that Tiggy's whiskers flickered, and the fluffy cat was definitely eyeing the bowls.

"I'll put the food here." Emma crouched down and stretched out her arm, trying to get the bowl into the stall without scaring Tiggy. "And Dad's got you some water too." She glanced across at her dad. "Can you see the kittens? Look, they haven't even got their eyes open!"

The kittens wriggled and made tiny mewing noises, calling for Tiggy to feed them. They were like little furry balloons, Emma thought, all plump and squidgy. Their fur was still quite short and fine, so the pink skin showed through on their tummies and paws, and their tails were almost as thin as string.

"I wish we could stay and watch," she murmured to Dad, as she edged away, still crouching. "But Tiggy might not want to eat while we're here because it'll mean leaving the kittens."

"I know, she is looking a bit worried," Dad agreed. "I love that little tabby. It looks like it's going to have great silver and black stripes. But they're all cute."

"I like that one too," Emma whispered, giving the kittens one last look from the doorway. "That's the sort of cat I've always imagined having."

Snuggled in the straw, the kittens cheeped faintly and blundered their way over towards their mother and her milk. They were so little that food and warmth were the only things they understood. They heard the soft vibrations of Emma's voice, and her dad's, but only Tiggy understood that Emma had brought her food and water, and had kept her distance from the precious kittens.

"The kitten of one of those cats at the stables?" Emma's mum asked doubtfully. "I don't think that's a very good idea, Emma. I know they look beautiful, but none of them are friendly. They're all half-wild. I don't think we want a cat like that." She put the salad on the kitchen table and sat down. "It isn't that I don't want us to have a pet, but we've never had a cat before. Shouldn't it be somebody who really knows what they're doing looking after kittens like those?"

"But there isn't anybody who knows!" Emma tried to argue. "Liz would be really pleased if we wanted to adopt one, I know she would. You should see him, Mum, the little grey tabby kitten. He's got white paws and white under his chin. His nose is all pink and soft because he's so small."

Mum smiled at her. "He sounds lovely, Emma. But a kitten like that might be a lot of work. Maybe we could find one from somewhere else?"

Emma looked desperately at her dad. She ought to be delighted – Mum had never said anything about being able to get a cat before. Emma knew that she was lucky to have her riding lessons – she'd never thought they'd be able to have a pet at home, too. But now she didn't want just any cat, she wanted to help those little kittens at the stables.

She'd always felt sorry for the stable cats, not having proper homes to go to. They didn't seem to mind – they curled up together in the stalls, and Liz put food out for them – but it wasn't like a lovely warm basket by the radiator, or sleeping at the end of someone's bed. She didn't want the kittens to grow up wild like their mother, even though Tiggy was gorgeous.

"Let's see what we can find out about taming kittens," Dad suggested. "They *were* very sweet. And I think it's too late to put Emma off them. She's already fallen in love with the little tabby. I wonder if it's a boy or a girl? We didn't get close enough to check."

"I thought he was a boy, just because he looked like he was wearing a little white shirt. But I don't know for sure."

Emma's dad looked over at her mum and she smiled.

"We'll see," Mum said. "I'm not promising anything, but perhaps you could do a bit of research. Find out what we'd have to do…"

"Yes!" Emma squealed. "Oh, Mum, this is so exciting! Please can we hurry up and eat lunch so I can look it all up on the computer."

"Hello, Ivy Bank Stables?"

"Hi, Liz," Emma said, a bit shyly. She'd never rung up the stables before – usually Mum did it if they had to book a lesson.

"Oh! Is that you, Emma? Is everything OK? How's your ankle?"

"It doesn't hurt at all now. I'm just ringing because I've been talking to Mum and Dad about the kittens. I asked if we could adopt one, but my mum's not sure. She says maybe it ought to be somebody who's more experienced with cats."

Emma frowned to herself, trying to remember all the information she and Dad had looked up that afternoon. "But the thing is, if they're going to be rehomed, the kittens need to have lots of contact with people, so they're not shy around humans like Tiggy and the others are. So I was wondering if I could come and spend some time with them."

"Yes, that makes sense," Liz said slowly. "And it's lovely that you want to help look after them, Emma. Of course you can – if your mum and dad are fine with it."

"Oh, they are," Emma told her. She hesitated, and then went on, "I'm really hoping Mum will let me adopt one of the kittens, if I can help tame them.

At the moment she's a bit worried that they'll be too wild. But we've found lots of ways to help with that. Me and Dad have been doing loads of research. It's the little tabby one I really love."

"He's adorable, isn't he? So is there anything I should be doing? Or the others at the stables?" Liz asked.

"I think just try to spend some time with them. Would it be OK if I came to the stables after school sometimes, as well as for my lessons? The more the kittens get used to people, the better. I'm guessing you want to find homes for the others as well?"

Emma heard Liz sigh down the phone. "Yes, I need to think about that. Perhaps I'll put a notice up on the board outside the stables."

"Oh!" Emma suddenly remembered something she'd read on a website. "There's a charity that'll help with neutering the cats. They'll even come and get them for you! They'll catch them and neuter them for free, and then bring them back."

"Really? That sounds amazing. Could you find their details for me, please?" Liz laughed. "You really are serious about cats, aren't you, Emma?"

Chapter Four

Emma went to the stables whenever she could get Mum or Dad to drive her. She spent most of her pocket money on a cat care book, just in case she did manage to persuade Mum to take the tabby kitten home. The kitten wouldn't be allowed to leave his mother until it was seven or eight weeks old, anyway. They had to give the kittens the chance to learn everything they needed from Tiggy. So she had plenty of time to read the whole book *and* persuade her mum that the tabby kitten would be the perfect pet.

The first time she went, Emma just sat quietly by the door. Tiggy watched her suspiciously, her ears laid back and the tip of her fluffy tail twitching. It was obvious that she was making Tiggy nervous, but she had to get to know the kittens, Emma told herself. It was so important. She wrapped her arms round her knees and just sat listening to the squeaks and rustles in the straw. By the time Dad came to pick her up, Tiggy was lying down feeding the kittens as if Emma wasn't there.

On her next visit, Emma decided to bring Tiggy some cat treats. If Tiggy was distracted, she might let Emma near the kittens. Liz had told her that Tiggy had licked the bowl of fish spotlessly clean, so Emma decided to get fish-flavoured ones.

She crouched down a little way from the kittens and shook some treats out of the packet next to Tiggy. The cat sniffed at them curiously. Emma could tell she wanted the fishy treats, but that

she wasn't ready to eat in front of her.
Emma sat with her chin on her knees,
looking away from Tiggy. Out of the
corner of her eye, she could just see her
edging closer to the pile.

Tiggy made one last little hop and
started to gobble down the treats.
Then she sniffed cautiously at Emma's
right foot – the part of her that was
nearest – and darted back to her
kittens. Emma couldn't stop herself
beaming. It felt like a breakthrough.

She opened the packet again,
making sure that Tiggy could hear it
rustle. Then she wriggled a bit closer,
shaking out a few more treats right
next to the cat. Emma really wanted to
get a proper look at the kittens, as she
thought they must be just over a week

old by now. She was hoping that their eyes would be open. Her cat book said that the kittens would all have blue eyes to begin with.

"They're definitely bigger," Emma whispered to Tiggy, who was still eating the treats. "They're beautiful." Tiggy looked up at Emma with her ears laid back and Emma sighed. "I know you don't like me talking. I don't want to scare you. I just want them to get used to hearing my voice. Anybody's voice, really."

Tiggy crunched the last fishy biscuit and Emma took a deep breath. She had stroked the cat a couple of times before, but not since she'd had the kittens. Slowly, she held out her hand to let Tiggy sniff it.

Tiggy dabbed her nose at Emma's hand cautiously, but she didn't hiss or raise the fur on her back. She actually looked quite calm. She rubbed her chin along Emma's wrist and then strolled back towards the kittens.

Emma held her breath and put the same hand down in the straw, next to the kittens. Tiggy lay down, stretched out beside her babies, and Emma smiled delightedly. She was almost touching them! And the little tabby was right next to her hand. Emma wondered if he could smell the fishy treats too, but she thought he was probably a bit young for that. His eyes were definitely open, though – just tiny blue slits. He looked like a teddy bear, with his round face and little triangle ears.

"I'm so lucky," Emma whispered, "getting to know you now when you're so small."

The kitten mewed squeakily and waved his front paws, wriggling closer to Emma. "I'm not your mum, small puss," she whispered. "I think you want to be over there. For some milk." Very gently she scooped him closer to Tiggy, so he could latch on and suckle. His fur was the softest thing she'd ever felt.

"I've got to think of a name," Emma muttered. "I can't keep just calling you small puss. Sam maybe? Or Sammy… You look like a Sammy. My little Sammy cat."

As the weeks went by, Sammy and the other kittens grew amazingly quickly. By four weeks they could all walk properly and suddenly they seemed to be interested in everything.

Tiggy spent a lot of her time trying to herd them back together, hurrying round them in the scattered straw and shooing them back to the nest. But as soon as she had one kitten safely tucked away, the other two would be padding out to explore again. Emma thought that Tiggy looked very tired. Liz had been putting down lots more food for her than usual, and Emma had been bringing her bowls of special cat milk and extra snacks, but it was hard work herding kittens and feeding them too.

The kittens were more like mini cats now – their heads still seemed much too big for their little bodies, but they'd lost their furry balloon look. They were really growing up.

"Hello," Emma whispered, crouching down by the door of the stall. Three little heads popped up at once and she giggled. They looked so funny, like the meerkats she'd seen at the zoo. Almost at once the tabby kitten plunged over the edge of the straw nest to come and see her.

"I've got something really special for you," Emma murmured. She and Liz had been talking about how they were going to wean the kittens – to get them eating food as well as Tiggy's milk. Emma had looked it up in her book, and Mum had got some baby rice and evaporated milk from the supermarket to mix up for the kittens. It looked a bit disgusting, but then Emma didn't much like the look of normal cat food either.

She'd bought a special litter tray as well, to put in the corner of the stall. According to her book, now that the kittens were trying solid food, they were going to poo a lot more too. Until now Liz had just scooped out the dirty straw every day.

Liz had said she'd be able to do most of the feeds and cleaning, and Alex and Sarah, who also taught at the stables, had said they could help as well. The kittens were going to need a bowl four times a day, so it was lucky Liz and the others were around.

"This is going to be yummy," Emma promised, dipping her finger in the white goo and holding it out to Sammy.

Sammy sniffed curiously and Emma rubbed the goo on his nose. He stepped back in surprise and sneezed. Then he licked at the dribbles of baby rice that were running down his muzzle. It was good! He licked harder, running his bright pink tongue all round his mouth and nose.

64

Sammy padded closer to the girl, hoping for some more of the white stuff. Emma was holding another splodge out for him and he licked it straight off her finger this time, trying to gobble it up fast. He could hear his brother and sister coming up behind him and he didn't want to share.

"Look," Emma murmured. "There's a whole bowlful…"

Sammy sniffed hopefully at the bowl and then started to lap hurriedly. The other two kittens appeared beside him and his sister plunged her face into the bowl eagerly. She came up smeared in white milky stuff, dripping from her nose and her black whiskers.

Emma laughed and all the kittens jumped, staring at her nervously.

"Sorry," she whispered softly.

Sammy watched her for a moment, then decided that she didn't mean any harm and went back to lapping. The food was so tasty, but it was making him sleepy, just like feeding from his mother did sometimes. He licked at the last smears at the bottom of the bowl and then licked his whiskers and yawned.

His brother and sister began to pad back towards their mother, to sleep curled up next to her, but the nest in the straw was a long way away. Sammy yawned again and eyed the girl. She was warm too – he knew it from the times she'd stroked him. He walked towards her, wobbling a bit, and tried to climb up her leg.

Emma looked at him, smiling in delighted surprise. Then she gently scooped a hand underneath his bottom and lifted him up on to her lap. Sammy flopped down, full and sleepy, and began a tiny purr.

"Oh, Emma," Mum whispered from the doorway. "Is that Sammy? You said it was the tabby one you really liked."

"Yes," Emma breathed. "He fell asleep on me. And he was purring, Mum."

"He is gorgeous," Mum said, smiling. "What does Tiggy think about him sleeping on you?"

Emma giggled. "She's asleep too.

I think she's grateful! She must be worn out looking after them all. I need to ask Liz if she's got something we can put across the doorway of the stall, a plank of wood maybe. So that Tiggy can get out but the kittens won't. Otherwise they'll be wandering all over the place soon. We might never find them!" She sighed. "I suppose we have to go, don't we?"

"We can hang on for a little bit. I don't want to make you move him. Why don't I go and ask Liz about finding something for the door?"

Emma nodded. Then, as her mum was turning to leave, she suddenly whispered, "Mum!"

"What is it? Is he waking up after all?"

"No, it's just … do you think we could adopt him? You said we had to see about having one of Tiggy's kittens – in case they were too wild."

Her mum looked down at Sammy, stretched out blissfully on Emma's knee. "He doesn't look very wild, does he?"

Emma shook her head, beaming.

Mum smiled at her. "All right then, we can adopt him. I'll tell Liz now."

Chapter Five

Keira stood by the door of the stall,
looking cautiously round it at Tiggy
and the dancing kittens. Emma had
managed to persuade her to come and
see them at last. They were playing
with a toy that Emma had bought
– a bundle of feathers on the end of
a long wire that she could flick and
wave about. The kittens loved it. They

stalked it, pounced on it, bounced around it, and all the while Tiggy sat watching them proudly. Every so often she couldn't resist and put out a paw to dab at the feathers too.

"They're so funny," Keira whispered to Emma. "I wish…"

"You could have a go," Emma suggested, holding out the toy.

Keira shook her head. "No," she said quickly. "It's OK."

Emma wanted to persuade her, but she had a feeling it would only make Keira feel worse. "I want to wear Sammy out a bit, before Dad comes and we put him in the carrying box," she explained. Dad was bringing the box when he came to pick Emma up from her lesson, any time now.

"Do you think Sammy won't like it?" Keira asked.

"I don't know." Emma sighed. "It feels mean taking him away from Tiggy and the other kittens, but he's about nine weeks old. Lots of kittens go to new homes then, even though it's a bit young. From the websites Dad and I looked at it sounded like it'd be best to rehome Sammy as soon as possible. Otherwise he'll do whatever his mum does. Tiggy still doesn't really like being touched and she'd never let me pick her up. I don't want Sammy to learn to be scared of people from her."

"What's going to happen to the other kittens?" Keira asked.

"Liz thinks she's found a lady who wants them," Emma said happily. "She's had cats before and she's going to take them both together. Later this week, I think." She glanced anxiously at Tiggy, who was still watching her kittens closely. "Poor Tiggy, she'll really miss them. But it is the best thing for the kittens, I'm sure it is."

"Oh! Your dad's here," Keira said, turning to look out of the barn door.

Emma let out an excited gasp. "Oh, wow…" she murmured. "I'm actually getting to take you home, Sammy!"

She had brought along a packet of cat treats, so they could tempt Sammy into the crate. The kittens were eating dry food like Tiggy now, although theirs was made for kittens. The cat treats were a special extra. Emma took the carrier from her dad and opened the wire door. Then she scattered a few treats inside. Tiggy and all the kittens edged closer – they knew what that rustling noise meant.

"They're all coming," Emma said worriedly to Dad.

"That's probably not a bad thing. We want Sammy to think the box isn't scary. If they all play around in it for a bit, he won't mind going in, will he?"

"I guess not." Emma watched as all three kittens explored their way around the carrier, nibbling at the treats and sniffing the soft cushion lining. Even Tiggy snapped up a treat that was just by the door.

"Emma, look," Dad murmured, a few minutes later. "Sammy's going in on his own. You can close the door in a second."

Emma nodded, and as the white tip of Sammy's striped tail cleared

the door, she gently swung it shut
and twisted the catches.

"Let's go home," she whispered.

Sammy sat pressed against the back
of the box. He had no idea what was
happening – he'd never seen anywhere
but the barn. Now he was shut into the
small, shadowy carrier and somehow it
was moving. The smells were strange
and sharp, and there was so much noise.
The vibration of the car was completely
new to Sammy and very frightening.

He could hear Emma's voice, and
her dad's, and he knew that they were
familiar, but it wasn't making him feel
much better.

"Do you think he's all right? I thought he might meow, but he's not even making any noise."

"It's a big shock for him, poor kitten. We're nearly back, Emma."

"We're almost home," Emma whispered through the holes in the carrier. "Not much longer."

Sammy felt himself pressed against the side of the carrier as the car swung round a corner. He let out a little hiss of fright and tried to back further into the box – but there wasn't anywhere to go. He scratched at the plastic, just a faint little movement of his paw. Nothing happened. Sammy closed his eyes and hoped his mother would come.

"I don't understand," Emma whispered. "He was so friendly before. He let me pick him up. He even slept on my lap."

"One of those websites did say to expect a kitten to take a couple of steps backwards when it's moved, Ems," Dad pointed out. "He's only been here a few hours."

"I didn't think he'd be this jumpy." Mum looked worriedly at Sammy, tense and nervous, his whiskers bristling.

"He's just a bit scared," Dad said encouragingly.

"I suppose so..." Mum sighed.

Emma looked over at the big wire crate they'd borrowed from one of the neighbours, whose puppy didn't need it any more. Sammy couldn't be loose in the house just yet, as he'd probably run off and hide. But they could put the crate on the table in the corner of the kitchen, and he could see everything that was going on and get used to lots of people being around. The kitchen didn't have any holes a kitten could get stuck in when they let him out to play.

It had seemed like the perfect plan for an almost-wild kitten. But Emma had imagined Sammy watching curiously as she ate her breakfast or did her homework. She'd thought of him purring to Dad as he made the dinner. She hadn't seen a hissing, spitting, miserable little kitten hiding at the back of his crate. He'd even swiped at her with his claws when she put a bowl of fresh water in for him. He'd missed, but still. It was like Sammy was a different kitten.

"We need to give him time," Dad said gently. "A day or so to calm down, before we start trying to handle him again."

"Yes," Emma sighed. "And I know I should have expected he wouldn't be very happy…" But she hadn't thought it would be like this. Mum looked so worried – and she'd really been coming round to the idea of a kitten!

What if she changed her mind?

Dad patted Emma's shoulder and then gave Mum a hug. "Don't look so tragic, you two! It'll be OK! I'm just going to make some coffee. Do you want anything, Emma?"

Emma shook her head. Deep down, she realized sadly, she'd just thought that Sammy would see how nice their house was. He'd know how excited she was to have a kitten of her own – he'd understand and he'd settle in straightaway.

"I was being stupid," Emma muttered to herself. She crouched down in front of the crate, looking at Sammy sideways. He was still huddled up at the back, his ears flat against his little head. "I thought everything would be perfect all at once. But I'll do anything to make you love us, Sammy. I just want you to be happy."

Chapter Six

Emma held out her fingers to Sammy. They were covered in roast chicken dinner baby food, which apparently was the most popular flavour with kittens. It felt sticky and gloopy, but she didn't mind. They'd given Sammy a whole twenty-four hours to calm down and Emma just couldn't wait any more. All the websites said that the way to make a half-wild kitten like you was to use food. They had to make Sammy see that food came from people and if he wanted the food he had to put up with them too.

"He's noticed, Ems," Dad breathed behind her. "He can smell it."

It was true. Emma could see Sammy's ears flickering, just a little. And his eyes were widening. "He must be able to smell it," she murmured. "It smells *disgusting*."

"Not to a cat," Dad whispered back.

"He's coming!" Emma tried not to sound too excited, or too loud. Sammy was stepping delicately, cautiously, across the crate to sniff at her fingers. His tiny pink tongue flicked out and he began to lick them.

Emma held her face straight, trying not to laugh and scare him away, but it tickled so much. His tongue was very strong for such a small kitten. And it was so rough. Emma leaned a little closer, so she could see the tiny white hairs all over his tongue. Sammy stopped licking and glanced worriedly up at her for a second. But then the deliciousness of the baby food won and he went back to getting every last bit out from under Emma's fingernails.

Emma wanted to pull her hand away to get some more from the jar, but she was sure that would frighten Sammy. Then she rolled her eyes. Of course! She dipped her other hand in, lifting out several fat fingerfuls, and slowly moved that hand into the crate too.

Sammy moved his head from side to side, as though he wasn't sure which hand to go for.

"Aww, poor Sammy – you've confused him now," Dad said.

Sammy decided that he couldn't get much more from Emma's right hand and changed to gulping down the food from her left. Emma looked at him thoughtfully. Her right hand was still in the crate. Very gently, she ran her hand down Sammy's back. He tensed a little, but he didn't spring away. Emma kept softly stroking his fur.

"Is that nice?" she whispered. "Is it nice being stroked, mmm?"

Sammy glanced up at her, as if to check what the noise was, but he kept licking.

"Keep stroking him," Dad murmured. "I'm going to get a little bowl of his proper dry food. Let's see if we can get him to eat that with us still here watching him."

He filled the bowl quietly and passed it to Emma so she could put it in front of Sammy. The little kitten darted back as the bowl suddenly appeared, but then he caught the scent of the dry cat food he was used to. He gave Emma's fingers one last hopeful swipe with his tongue and moved on to the bowl.

"You try stroking him," Emma whispered to Dad.

Dad nodded and reached slowly into the crate, running one finger down Sammy's back as he busily gobbled the food. Sammy glanced over his shoulder, but he didn't stop eating.

"It really works," Dad murmured. "We can do this again when we feed him at lunchtime."

Emma nodded. "Every time we feed him. And maybe soon we can get him out of the crate and let him eat from his bowl on the floor." She sighed happily. "It's really going to be OK, Dad, I'm sure it is."

"Which top do you think I should wear?" Mum held two out on hangers.

"Mmm. The black one," Emma said, watching Sammy. He'd nearly finished his bowl of food and he was looking sleepy. She had her arm inside his cage, with her hand cupped round him. Emma had a feeling he might fall asleep with her hand still there, which would be brilliant. He'd be almost back to the same friendly Sammy she'd known at the stables, and it was only a week since they'd brought him home.

"Are you sure?" Mum frowned. "You didn't look for very long…"

"Yes, Mum. I can stroke Sammy *and* look, you know. Hurry up! Auntie Grace'll be here to babysit soon."

Mum rushed off, and Emma giggled and gently moved the food bowl. Sammy had fallen asleep with his head in it! He twitched a little and then flopped down, collapsing across her hand with a little wheezy snore. She leaned against the crate, closing her eyes and smiling dreamily to herself. Soon they'd be able to take him out of there and he'd be a real pet, she was sure.

90

"Are you asleep, Emma?"

"Oh! Auntie Grace, shh. I'm not, but Sammy is." Emma reached out the arm that wasn't in the crate to hug her aunt. "I didn't hear you come in."

"Your dad was walking up the path when I pulled up, so I didn't have to ring the bell. He's just gone to change. So this is Sammy? He's gorgeous."

"Isn't he?" Emma agreed proudly. "And he's getting much more confident again. He was really upset on Saturday when we brought him home, but he's a lot happier now." Carefully, she slid her hand out from underneath him, and Sammy snuffled but stayed asleep. She grinned at her aunt. "I've got pins and needles now. Mum says please can you help me with my science homework, but she's got us a DVD for afterwards."

Emma yawned and snuggled against Auntie Grace. "Can't we watch a bit more?"

"No! You know your mum said eight-thirty, cheeky. Besides, haven't you got to feed Sammy before bed?"

"Oh yes, and you haven't seen him awake yet, I forgot!" Emma sprang up from the sofa. "I'll go and get his food." She hurried into the kitchen and began to measure it out, while Sammy padded up and down the crate, watching her and mewing hopefully.

Emma had just opened the door

of the crate to put the bowl in when Auntie Grace pushed open the kitchen door. It banged slightly and Sammy jumped at the noise. He saw Auntie Grace – someone he'd never met before – and suddenly panicked. He hissed loudly and Emma stared at him. "What's the matter, Sammy?"

"Oh dear, is he OK?" Auntie Grace asked, leaning over to look at him.

Sammy hissed again as he saw the strange person coming closer. He darted out of the crate door, desperate to get away.

"I think he's a bit scared because you're new," Emma said worriedly, trying to catch him. "Maybe you'd better just let me sort him out, Auntie Grace."

Auntie Grace stepped back out of the kitchen, but Sammy was already spooked. He scrabbled over Emma's arm in a panic, accidentally clawing at her wrist so that she squeaked and dropped the food bowl.

The bowl smashed on the tiles with a huge crash, and Sammy yowled in fright. He raced round the side of the crate, but the table was pushed up against the wall below the window and there was nowhere to go. Frantically, he clawed his way up the curtains, digging his tiny claws into the fabric.

Sammy hung there, swaying a little. He didn't really understand what had happened. He'd been about to eat his food – he could smell it – and then suddenly everything was different and terrifying. Now he didn't even know where he was, or how he'd got so high up.

The curtain fabric ripped a little under his weight and he slid down a few centimetres with a frightened mew. He tried to claw his way back up again, but the shiny fabric was difficult to climb and he slipped further down.

"Sammy, it's all right…" Emma's voice, low and soothing. And now he wasn't falling any more. Her hands were around him, the way they were when she fed him sometimes. After struggling for a moment, he let her unhook his paws from the few last threads of the curtains and sat tensely in her hands, ears back and fur fluffed up. She lifted him down, still whispering gently, and slid him back into the crate. Sammy backed away from the door anxiously, but the strange person had gone now, he could see. It was just Emma. He knew her. She was safe.

Chapter Seven

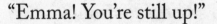

"Emma! You're still up!"

Emma jerked awake. Mum was standing in the living-room doorway, looking surprised.

"Sorry," said Auntie Grace. "Emma was upset, I didn't want to make her go to bed…"

"What happened?" Dad asked, just at the same time as Mum noticed

Emma's scratched wrist and swooped down to check it.

"Emma, you've hurt yourself! Oh no, was it Sammy?"

"He didn't mean to." Emma looked sleepily at Dad and Mum. "It was an accident. And, um, I broke his food bowl. Sorry… We swept it up."

"What's been going on?" Dad sat down on the arm of the sofa and Mum came to sit next to Emma.

Emma sighed. She was so tired it was hard to explain. "I went to feed him but he was scared of Auntie Grace."

"It was my fault. I should have thought, of course, he's never seen me before," Auntie Grace put in. "And he's a bit more nervous than most kittens. I frightened him and he jumped out of the crate and scratched Emma by accident."

"And that made me drop his bowl, and he got even more scared and ran up the curtains."

"Oh my goodness," Mum muttered.

"I'm afraid he did tear them a bit," Auntie Grace went on slowly. "But he's back in the crate now and he's calmed down. In fact, last time Emma checked he was asleep, wasn't he?"

Emma nodded.

Mum leaned back against the sofa and let out a huge sigh. "I knew this was a mistake. We should never have brought him home. He was so upset when we took him away from the stables and his mum. I just don't think it's fair."

"Mum!" Emma gasped.

"Oh, Emma. You have to see I'm right – just look at your wrist!"

Emma looked down at the three long red lines and the little scratches that she'd got all over her hands when she was taking Sammy off the curtains. They were sore but it hadn't been Sammy's fault. He was just scared – he hadn't meant to hurt her.

Mum put her arm round Emma. "I know how hard you've tried with Sammy, but he might not be the right cat for us after all. He needs to go to a shelter, I think. Where they've got people who are used to looking after cats like him."

"I'm not sure," Dad said. "I know Sammy was difficult when we brought him home, but he is getting better."

"Getting better!" Mum stared at him. "Emma's covered in scratches!"

"I don't think it's that big a deal," Auntie Grace said gently. "Even Whisky scratches me sometimes, if I go to pick him up and he just doesn't feel like it."

Mum sighed again. "I'm sorry, Emma, but he's too unpredictable. I'm not sure he's ever going to be really friendly. Maybe he needs a home more like the stables, where he doesn't have to be around people if he doesn't want to."

"Mum, please don't send him away!" Emma wailed. "I don't want any other cat, only Sammy! He'll be fine, he will. I'll do anything to keep him." She stared pleadingly at her mum, tears trickling down her cheeks. She couldn't bear the thought of poor Sammy going to a shelter – somewhere else strange and new and frightening. He'd have to start all over again and soon it would be too late to tame him. He'd be shy and wild forever.

"Look, just give us a few more weeks, love," Dad suggested. "Of course today's a bit of a setback, but we have to keep trying."

"Two more weeks." Mum looked from Emma to Dad and back again. "We have to be able to tell by then, don't we?"

Dad nodded slowly. "All right. Emma?"

"I suppose so," Emma whispered huskily. She was so upset her voice seemed to have disappeared. Two weeks! It was no time at all.

"What's the matter?" Keira asked, as she led Jasmine past Emma and Sparky. "Is Sparky being a pain about getting tacked up again? You look, well, a bit sad…" she trailed off, not sure what to say. Emma looked like she might be about to cry.

"No." Emma sniffed. "Actually Sparky's been a total star. Maybe he can tell I just can't deal with a tricksy pony today."

"Oh no, what is it?" Keira swapped Jasmine's reins to her other hand and gave Emma a hug. "Don't cry!"

"I can't help it." Emma's voice shook. "Mum says we might have to give Sammy to a shelter. She thinks we can't cope with him."

"But wasn't it going really well?" Keira said, confused. "You showed me that photo your dad took of him eating off your fingers. He looked so happy."

"He's still jumpy, though," Emma gulped. "Mum thinks he's not going to adapt to living in a house. He got scared last night because my auntie was there and he scratched me. I didn't mind – not much – but Mum was really upset about it. She says we've got two weeks to prove he can be a proper pet, or he has to go." She could hardly get the last words out, she was crying so much.

Keira hugged her tighter, and even Sparky and Jasmine leaned in close, as if they wanted to make Emma feel better.

"Two weeks is a long time," Keira said. "Honestly, it really is. And I saw how friendly and tame he was with you here. You nearly had *me* stroking him, Emma, and I'm scared of cats!"

"I suppose so…" Emma said, between gasps. "It doesn't feel like long, though. If he goes to a shelter he'll be all lost and alone. It'll be awful."

"Then you absolutely have to make sure it doesn't happen," Keira said firmly. "I'll see if I can think of anything to help." She gave Emma one last hug. "Ems, we have to go. Liz is waving at us. She wants us to try those dressage aids today, remember?"

Emma nodded and sniffed hard. "I'm OK. I'm so glad I told you about it, Keira. I do actually feel a bit happier."

Emma grabbed her riding hat from
the back seat and looked anxiously
at Auntie Grace's purple car parked
outside their house.

"It's all right," Dad said soothingly.
"She said she wouldn't go near Sammy.
Although we will have to try and
get him used to meeting new people
eventually. She's got something for
you."

Emma hurried down the path,
curious to see what Auntie Grace
had brought. She had a feeling it was
something important – not just a
magazine or some chocolate to cheer
her up, but something that really
mattered.

"Emma! I'm so glad you got back before I had to go to work. Look, I've brought you this." Auntie Grace whirled out of the front door on to the path. "Here. I really hope it helps."

Emma looked down at the book that her aunt had pressed into her hands – *Taming Feral Kittens*. There was a gorgeous little ginger kitten on the front of it, with a shy, worried look on his face that made Emma think of Sammy at once.

"I got it at the animal shelter. I thought I'd go and ask them if they had any tips for you. They were so friendly and helpful. This was written by someone who used to work there and they said to call if you get really stuck. I wrote the number inside the cover for you." She hugged Emma. "Sweetheart, if Sammy does have to go there, they will look after him, I promise."

Emma nodded. "But it's not going to happen," she said firmly. "This is brilliant, Auntie Grace. I'm going to go and read it now."

Sammy sat in the doorway of the crate, looking out suspiciously. Everything was different – the crate had been moved down on to the floor, and he didn't like that, for a start. He preferred to be high up, so he could see who was coming. High up was safe.

But he liked the open door. He thought he did, anyway. He sniffed the air beyond the crate, his whiskers twitching. He could step out, right on to the floor. He could explore. Cautiously, he extended one paw over the door frame, and then the next, and then his two back paws.

He stood nervously just outside the crate, watching, scanning the room. Emma was there, sitting in the corner, and her dad was over by the counter. She wasn't looking at him – she was gazing off into the distance as if she hadn't noticed what he was doing. Sammy took a few steps out into the room and sniffed.

Food! He could definitely smell food. He was sure it was well past his usual feeding time. He'd been expecting Emma to bring food, but instead she and her dad had lifted his crate down on to the floor. Determinedly, he stomped across the floor, towards the smell. Emma had his bowl on her lap. He stopped a few steps away from her, looking uncertainly at the bowl. He wasn't sure he wanted to go any closer, but he was hungry.

His tail swished from side to side, and then he made a panicked little run, flinging himself at the bowl. What if she took it away? Sammy climbed up on Emma's leg and started to gobble down the food as quickly as he could.

"It's all right," Emma murmured. "I'm not going anywhere."

Sammy's ears flickered but he didn't stop eating. Then he felt her stroking him, very gently running her hand over his shoulders and down his back. It was nice – it felt like his mother licking him. He slowed his eating down a little, almost sure that the bowl wasn't going to be taken away.

At last, he'd finished the whole bowl. He licked round it carefully and then sniffed it to make sure there wasn't any more. There wasn't, but he was full anyway.

Slowly, carefully, he settled down into a crouch on Emma's lap. She was still stroking him, so gently. Sammy stretched out his paws and kneaded them up and down on Emma's skirt. Then he closed his eyes and purred.

Chapter Eight

Emma tucked the phone under her chin so she could talk to Auntie Grace and have both hands free for scrabbling after the ping-pong ball as Sammy sent it skittering around all over the floor.

"It really works," she told her aunt, a little breathlessly. "We started on Sunday after I'd had time to read the book. All this week, we've only fed him with the bowl on me or Dad, so that he has to come to us to get his food. And he's always hungry, so it works perfectly. The very first time we tried it, he let me stroke him and he even purred! I'm starting to think he actually does like me," she added shyly.

"Of course he does. Oh, that's wonderful, Emma! I felt awful when your mum said you might have to give him up."

"Me too. But I'm so hoping she's going to let me keep him. She was laughing at him this morning, when he was playing with his feathery toy before school. He kept almost falling over backwards, he was trying so hard to catch it." Emma threw the ping-pong ball again for Sammy. "We're doing the next thing it says in the book now. He's going to be allowed out in the kitchen all the time, not just for food time and playing. His bed and his litter tray are still in the crate, but we'll leave it open so he can come and go when he wants to."

"And then I suppose you'll bring his bed out and eventually get rid of the crate?"

"Exactly. I don't know how long it's going to take, though. The book says it depends on the kitten. Oh, Sammy!"

"What did he do?" Auntie Grace laughed at the other end of the line.

"He chased after the ball so fast he ran into the cupboard. He's fine, he just looks a bit confused. One minute." Emma laid the phone on the floor and wriggled closer to Sammy, murmuring comforting noises. She was sure that he looked embarrassed, if a kitten could. His ears had gone flat.

"It's OK," she whispered and without thinking about it, she scooped Sammy gently into her hands and snuggled him up against her cardigan. "Oh… I didn't mean to…" It was the first time she'd ever picked him up. But Sammy hadn't clawed her or jumped away in fright. He was huddled against her, so tiny and fragile that she could feel his heart beating under her fingers. "You don't mind?" she murmured. "Oh, Sammy, I do love you…"

"Hey…" Dad whispered from the doorway. "He looks happy!"

"Dad, can you pick up the phone?"

Emma whispered. "I was talking to Auntie Grace. She must be wondering what happened to me. Can you tell her I'll call her later?"

Dad chuckled. "Sure. I'll tell her you're occupied with some very important business."

"Are you sure?" Emma looked worriedly at Keira. "I mean, I'd love it if you came over for lunch. But I know how you feel about cats."

"Exactly," Keira called back, as she hefted Jasmine's saddle over to the tackroom. "And so does your mum. So if even silly Keira isn't scared of playing with Sammy, he must be OK as a pet, mustn't he? The two weeks are up, aren't they? We need to show your mum how good Sammy is."

"Two weeks yesterday. I haven't wanted to ask Mum what's happening." Emma sighed. "And I never said you were silly," she added quickly.

Keira grinned. "I know. But I am silly.

I can't even say what it is that makes me frightened of cats. They just make me so nervous."

"I don't want you to be miserable." Emma frowned. "And…" She nibbled her bottom lip. "If you're nervous it might make Sammy nervous too," she explained. "He was all right with Auntie Grace when she came over in the week. She was really good, she just sat on the floor completely still until he was brave enough to sniff at her. But she's used to cats and she wasn't scared."

"I won't be scared, either," Keira said. "I promise. I said I'd try to think of something I could do to help, and this is it. I'll be brave." She smiled at Emma. "Honestly. I'll be fine."

"He's in here, in the kitchen." Emma looked back at Keira. She could see her mum hovering behind her friend, with an anxious expression on her face. Mum obviously wasn't sure about this – neither was Emma, to be honest. But Keira seemed so certain. She'd explained to Emma's mum in the car that she wanted to try and stop being scared of cats, and that she knew she'd be OK with Sammy because he was so little.

Emma opened the door slowly and peered round. "Oh, he's asleep in his basket. Actually, that's good. How about we sit on the floor for a bit? We can have a snack, and then when he wakes up we can let him come and see you."

Keira nodded. She was quite pale, Emma thought. But she looked determined too. "That's a good idea."

Emma took her hand, pulling her gently into the kitchen to sit down half under the table. That would give Sammy plenty of space to look at them properly before he got out of his basket. Keira even giggled when Emma's mum handed them a plate of cheese cubes and apple to eat under there. "It's like being really small and making tents under the table. Did you ever do that?" she whispered.

"Yes! Hey, I think he's waking up." Emma glanced at her. "Sure you're all right?"

"Mm-hm."

Emma could feel Keira tensing up beside her. Maybe it *was* a stupid idea, after all. But it was too late to do anything about it now.

Sammy stretched and yawned, and popped his head up out of his basket to see what was happening. He was hungry and he could smell something delicious. Not his normal food, but that only made it more exciting. He twitched his ears forwards and gazed at Emma under the table. Emma and someone else. He flicked his tail from side to side worriedly. It wasn't someone he knew, but she was sitting quite still. She had some of whatever it was that smelled so nice, he could see it in her hands. And she was holding it very close to the floor…

Sammy hopped out of his basket and set off across the floor, his whiskers trembling as he smelled the cheese. He nudged his head against

Emma's feet on the way, as if to say
that she belonged to him. But he was
still more interested in the cheese. He
padded between Emma's legs and the
new girl's, and sniffed hopefully at the
girl's fingers. She was holding that
piece of cheese as if she didn't really
want it at all.

He froze for a second,
ears flickering, expecting
someone to shoo him
away. But no one did.
Swiftly, Sammy
swooped the scrap
out of her hand
and gulped
it down,
savouring
every crumb.

125

Then he licked Keira's fingers, just
to check he hadn't missed any. He felt
her laugh – her fingers shook – but
there was no more cheese. He gave her
one last lick, and turned to scramble
up into Emma's lap. He could still
smell cheese, and he was sure that if
Emma had any, she'd give it to him.
He hauled himself up her leggings,
breathing hard, and half fell into her
lap. Then he sat
there and gave a
massive yawn,
showing
all his tiny
sharp teeth
and his
raspberry-
pink tongue.

"He's gorgeous," Keira whispered, sounding quite surprised.

"You didn't mind when he licked you?" Emma asked. She couldn't stop smiling – Sammy had perched himself on her lap like he belonged.

Keira wrinkled her nose. "Actually, I was really scared. But he's so little – I just kept thinking I could run out if I couldn't deal with it."

"Oh, Keira," Emma's mum murmured. "Do you want to go into the other room?"

Keira shook her head. "No, I think it's OK," she said cautiously. "He's really good."

Emma's mum nodded. "I suppose he is." She smiled at Emma. "So are you having lunch under the table, then?"

"I don't think we'd actually get much of our lunch if we did that." Slowly, carefully, Emma moved on to her knees, cuddling Sammy against her fleece top as she stood up and went to sit on one of the kitchen chairs. She was waiting for him to leap away, but Sammy only stretched his neck out so he could peer over the edge of the table at the plate of sandwiches that her mum was putting down.

Keira laughed. "He's eyeing the food as though you never feed him, Emma."

"He needn't think he's making a habit of sitting on your lap at mealtimes," Mum said sternly. "Just this once."

Emma stared at her delightedly.

"You mean…"

Her mum nodded. "Yes – I was talking to your dad about it last night. Sammy's so much happier now. Oh, Emma, watch out, he's going for that ham sandwich!" She quickly pulled the plate back and Sammy looked disappointed.

"I'll get you a bit in a minute," Emma whispered in his ear. "A whole sandwich, if you like!"

Sammy yawned again and purred a little and rubbed his face against her hand. Then he nuzzled at Emma's top and pawed his way gently over the zip, snuggling down inside.

Emma looked down lovingly at the little tabby kitten curled up inside her fleece. "Sammy, you're staying!"

The
Secret
Kitten

For Poppy and Star, my not-so-secret kittens…

Chapter One

Lucy stood on tiptoe with her elbows balanced on the windowsill, leaning out to look down at the garden. She had never had a room like this before, right up at the very top of the house. She was so high up that the garden looked strange and far below, the trees short and stubby, even though she knew that they were tall.

Actually, she had never had a room of her own before. She had always shared with William, her little brother. But now they were living at Gran's house, there was space for each of them to have their own room. It was lovely and really odd, both at the same time.

Lucy had mixed feelings about everything at the moment. Gran's house was beautiful with a big garden, not like the tiny garden she'd had back home, but she couldn't stop thinking about the old house. They had been to Gran's loads of times, of course, but always as visitors. Living there was going to be strange and different. The house didn't feel like it was their home yet, even though Dad had explained that he'd bought half of it from Gran. They were all going to share. Gran would help look after Lucy and William, and Dad would sort out the wild, overgrown garden that had got too much for Gran recently, and they would all be company for each other.

It would be good for Dad, Lucy thought, resting her chin on her hands as she stared down at the trees. For the last five years, ever since their mum had died, he'd looked after her and William by himself. He'd had a little help from childminders, but mostly he had been in charge of everything. Now he would have Gran to help and maybe he wouldn't be so worried all the time. It was hard when he had to stay late at work and missed picking up Lucy and William from after-school clubs, or the childminder, or their friends' houses.

Lucy swallowed hard. They wouldn't be going back to their after-school clubs. They weren't even going back to their old school – Gran's house was too far away. On Monday, she and

William would be starting all over again at a new school. Lucy wasn't looking forward to it.

"It'll be all right," Lucy whispered to herself. "It was nice when we went to see it." The teacher had been friendly and smiley, William had loved the big climbing frame in the playground and it was only a five-minute walk from Gran's house. But it was new and different, and even though there would be a coat peg ready with her name on it and a drawer for her books in the classroom, Lucy knew she didn't really belong there, not yet.

Something stirred among the trees. Lucy squinted sideways, trying to work out what it was. A bird? Then she smiled. A large ginger cat was walking carefully along the fence, padding from paw to paw, slow and stately. *He must belong next door,* Lucy thought. Gran didn't have a cat. She didn't have any pets, even though this would be the perfect house for one with its lovely big garden. Lucy thought Gran's beautifully tidy living room would look a lot nicer with a cat draped along the back of the sofa, or curled up on the rug.

But Dad had told them that Gran didn't like pets. She thought they were too messy, and caused fuss and dirt and work. Lucy wished she could argue with Gran and say what about purring and how a cat could keep your feet warm on a cold night? But you couldn't start that sort of an argument with your gran – not her gran, anyway. She wasn't an arguing sort of person. Lucy loved her, but Gran was one of those people who knew she was always right. And she was the one who would be doing most of the tidying up too!

"Lucy!"

It was William! Lucy spun round, hearing the wobbly tearful note in his voice. "What's the matter?" she asked worriedly.

"Gran shouted at me," William
sniffed. He sat down on the floor,
leaning against Lucy's bed. His face
was muddy, except for two little trails
where tears had run down.

"Why?" Lucy sat next to him and
put her arm round his shoulders.

William snuggled into her. "I was
playing football in the garden and then
I brought the ball back in with me and
I bounced it…"

"Oh, William! Where?" Lucy
demanded and he edged away from her
a little, hunching his shoulders up.

"In the living room."

"You didn't break anything, did you?" Lucy asked anxiously. Dad had made them promise to be careful, but William was only six and sometimes he just forgot things like that.

"No!" William protested indignantly. "But Gran was still really cross. She said I wasn't to kick balls around in the house, but I hadn't even kicked it! I was just bouncing it." He sighed and leaned back on her shoulder again, peering around Lucy's room at the cardboard boxes, already nearly all unpacked.

"Do you like having your own bedroom?" he whispered seriously.

Lucy nodded. "Yes… But last night I missed hearing you talking to your

Lego people," she added, to make him feel better.

"I do like my bedroom." William didn't sound so sure. "But do you think I could keep all my things in my room, then sleep up here with you? I could bring my sleeping bag."

"Maybe sometimes," Lucy said comfortingly. It had been strange going to bed last night without William snoring and snuffling on the other side of the room, but she was glad to have a place that was just her own.

All her own, except that it would be so nice to share it with a cat. *Any cat*, Lucy thought, wondering if the big ginger cat from next door ever came to visit.

Chapter Two

The black-and-white kitten peered around the pile of old boxes. Her ears were laid back flat and her tail was twitching. Out in the alleyway between the baker's shop and newsagent, she could see her brother and sister frisking about, chasing each other and wrestling. Her paws itched to join in. She stepped out a little further.

Then a car roared past on the main road and she darted back into her hiding place in the storage yard. Seconds later, her tabby brother and sister shot back in after her and they all huddled together in the dark little corner, hissing at the strange, frightening noise. The two tabby kittens wriggled and stamped their paws inside a broken packing case, making themselves comfy on the old rags and torn-up papers, trying to find the warmest, driest spot. The black-and-white kitten licked them both lovingly, hoping that they'd all curl up together and snooze, as they waited for their mother to come back from her foraging. But the tabby kittens didn't want to hide for long. A minute or so later they were already nosing out into the alleyway again.

Their little sister watched them anxiously, wondering about that loud noise and hoping that whatever it was wouldn't come back. The alleyway was so open – she liked places where she could hide and still see everything. All that space made her nervous.

"Oh, look! Kittens!"

A little boy came running into the alleyway and the tabby kittens streaked back towards the old boxes, knocking their black-and-white sister sideways. She huddled at the back of their little den, her heart thumping, but the bravest of the tabbies was too curious to stay hidden, even with the boy blundering around, his feet stamping and thudding. She scrambled out past the broken board on to the top of the box and gazed at him.

"Mum, look…" the little boy whispered. "It really is a kitten! She's tiny!"

"Isn't she? She's gorgeous."

The black-and-white kitten squeaked worriedly. There was someone else out there too. She wished her sister would come back, but now her brother was wriggling out to see what was going on.

"Oh, there's two! Look, Owen, the other one's come out to see you. I wonder who they belong to. I suppose they're strays, but they look very young. Their mother must be around somewhere."

The voices were soft and gentle, and the black-and-white kitten stretched her paws, shook her whiskers and began to creep towards the opening. Perhaps she would go and see what was happening.

But then the little boy shrieked with laughter, as kitten whiskers tickled his fingers. The kitten ran back and buried herself among the rags again. At last she heard their footsteps echoing back down the alleyway and she relaxed a bit. Then a tabby-striped face pushed in through the gap between the boxes and she darted forwards to nuzzle happily at her mother. The thin tabby cat had been hiding out of the way until the little boy and his mum had gone. She had always been a stray and she wasn't very fond of people. People meant food, but sometimes they threw things and shouted at her for scrabbling around in bins. She avoided them as much as she could.

The tabby kittens piled in after her and tore at the ham sandwich she'd found for them, scrapping and hissing over the delicious pieces of ham. The kittens were eight weeks old and they were all still drinking her milk as well as eating food, but they were always hungry.

The black-and-white kitten finished her piece of sandwich and snuggled luxuriously up against her mother. She was warm and safe and full of food. Her brother and sister flopped down on top of her in a softly purring pile of fur and all four of them curled up to sleep.

"So, what was it like?" Gran asked, smiling at Lucy, as they walked home from school on Monday. She didn't need to ask how school had been for William. He was bouncing around the pavement in front of them with his new best friend, Harry, doing ninja kicks.

"It was all right," Lucy said, not very enthusiastically. It was true. No one had been mean and she'd understood the work they were doing. Emma, the girl who'd been told to look after her, had been nice and had made sure she knew where everything was.

But she'd stayed on the sidelines of all the games. And everyone knew secret jokes about the teachers that she didn't and there was no one who knew all the fun things about her, the things her friends back home knew. She was just a rather boring new girl.

Gran put an arm round her shoulders. "It'll get better, Lucy, I promise. In a month's time, it won't feel like a new school any more."

Lucy blinked. She hadn't expected Gran to notice that she wasn't really happy. "I suppose so," she murmured and smiled gratefully at Gran.

"Why don't we stop in at the baker's and get a treat? To celebrate school being just about all right?" Gran suggested.

William turned round mid-air and came racing back to them, saying goodbye to Harry. "Cakes? Can we?

Can I have a marshmallow ice cream?"

Gran made a face. "I suppose so. I don't know how you can eat those things, though."

"It's really easy," William told her solemnly and Lucy giggled, feeling the nervous lump inside her melt away for the first time that day.

It was as they were coming out of the baker's shop, each clutching a rustling paper bag, that Lucy first saw the kittens. She wondered afterwards if they'd heard the bags crinkling, and were hoping that she and William might drop some food.

She'd seen a flash out of the corner of her eye, a darting movement in the alleyway. Lucy almost didn't stop to look at first – she'd thought that it was probably just pigeons, hopping about after crumbs – but then something had made her turn back and look properly.

The soft grey shadows peering out behind the bins had been cats!

No, kittens. Tiny kittens, two of them, their green eyes round and huge in little striped faces.

Lucy reached out her hand to grab at William, who was explaining very seriously to Gran that it was important to eat a marshmallow cone from the bottom up, as then you got to save the marshmallow for last.

"Ow! What?"

"Look…" Lucy whispered, pulling him closer so that he'd see. "But shh!"

"What am I looking at and you didn't have to grab me, Lucy, Dad says— Oh!"

Gran peered over their heads. "Please tell me that's not a rat."

"They're kittens, Gran. Can we go and take a closer look? Please?"

Gran looked at the shops on

either side of the alleyway. "Well, I shouldn't think they'll mind. Don't go into the yard, though, and don't touch them."

Lucy and William crept down the alley, holding hands. The little tabby kittens stared at them from behind the wheelie bins. They were crouched low to the ground, ready to spring away to safety, but they stayed still as the children came closer.

When they were almost at the bins, Lucy kneeled down, gently pulling William with her.

"Can't we go closer?" he begged.

"Not yet," she whispered back. "When I went to Jessie's house, her cat was really shy and I had to sit like this for ages, but then he climbed into my lap and let me cuddle him. Jessie says he never does that." Suddenly, Lucy was blinking away tears, thinking of Jessie and all her friends back home.

"They're coming closer." William poked her arm impatiently. "Look!"

Lucy dragged her hand across her eyes. It was true – one of the kittens had padded all the way out now – he was almost close enough to sniff at William's outstretched fingers.

Then, all at once, he darted forwards and dabbed his nose at William's hand.

William squeaked delightedly, "His nose is all cold and damp!"

The kitten disappeared back behind the bins in a blur.

"Sorry!" William whispered.

But it only took seconds for the kitten to be brave enough to peek out again and this time the other tabby kitten followed him, sniffing curiously at Lucy's school shoes.

Very slowly, Lucy reached out and stroked the kitten's stripey head with the tips of her fingers – the fur was so soft, almost silky. And then the kitten purred, so loudly that Lucy couldn't help giggling. The noise seemed too big for such a tiny creature.

"I wonder where their mother is," Lucy murmured to William, looking down the alley to see if the mother cat was watching them playing with her babies.

"Are they lost?" William asked worriedly.

"No," Gran said quietly behind them. "I was just talking to Emma – the girl from the baker's. She said that they live in the yard – there's a pile of old boxes and things. She's been putting some food down for them."

"They live in a *box*?" Lucy said, thinking how cold it had been the night before.

Gran nodded. "Yes. But apparently a couple of her regular customers are thinking of trying to adopt these two, once they're big enough to leave their mother. That won't be long."

"Gran, there's another one!" Lucy gasped. "I was looking for their mum, but there's a kitten peeping out of that old box! A black-and-white one!"

"So there is!" Gran looked over to where Lucy was pointing. "That's odd, the lady in the shop only mentioned the two tabbies. Maybe that little one isn't as friendly as the others. I'm sorry, you two, we have to be off. I need to get dinner ready." She smiled down at Lucy's disappointed face. "I'm sure they'll still be here tomorrow…"

Chapter Three

They were late the next morning, because William had spilled half a bowl of cereal down his school uniform, so there was no time to stop and play with kittens. Lucy looked down the alleyway hopefully on their way to school, but she couldn't see even a whisker. She imagined all the kittens having a lie-in, curled up snugly in their old box.

When they stopped on the way home, Emma, the lady from the baker's, was there, putting some rubbish out in the bins. She smiled at Lucy and William and said, "Are you looking for those kittens? I'm really sorry, that lady I was telling your gran about came and took them home with her this morning."

"Oh…" Lucy swallowed. William's eyes had filled with tears and she felt like crying too. She nudged her little brother. "That's good," she said firmly, trying to convince herself as well as William. "It's getting colder now it's autumn. Imagine sleeping outside in a box all winter."

Gran nodded. "It would be horrible. Damp and chilly. They're much better off with a nice home indoors."

"I know." William sniffed. "But I wanted to see them. We only got to see them once."

"I'll miss them," Emma said, as Lucy and William turned to go. "Cute little pair. Gorgeous stripes."

Lucy glanced back at her. "But – there was a black-and-white kitten too. Did she take all three of them?"

Emma blinked. "Three? Really? I thought there were only two of them."

"No." Lucy shook her head. "Definitely three. We saw the black-and-white one yesterday."

"She's right," Gran put in. "I saw her too. She reminded me of the cat I had when I was a little girl, called Catkin. This kitten had the same lovely white tip on her tail."

Lucy glanced at William in surprise. Gran had had a cat of her own? But she didn't like pets, Dad had said.

William wasn't really listening, though. "Gran, is the little kitten left all on her own now?"

"Her mum's still there," Emma pointed out.

"No other kittens to play with, though," Lucy said sadly.

William beamed at her. "Maybe she'll come and play with us instead, then, if she's lonely." He ran a few steps further down the alley and called, "Puss! Puss! Kitten!"

"She won't come out if you yell at her," Lucy said. "We've got to be gentle. Maybe tempt her out. Could we buy some cat treats, Gran?"

"I suppose so." Gran nodded. "Maybe if that kitten gets a bit more used to people, someone will take her home too."

Lucy caught her breath. She almost asked Gran if they could be the ones to give the kitten a home. But then she remembered everything Dad had said about having to keep the house tidy and not damaging Gran's lovely things and how Gran hated mess. And then she thought about Jessie's mum rolling her eyes and sighing and saying, "Oh, not again!" when Jessie's cat Socks had knocked a vase of flowers off the kitchen table.

There was no way Gran would let them have a cat, even if the kitten did look like her old pet, Catkin.

Lucy frowned down at her magazine.
It was her favourite one, a pet
magazine that she got every week.
She'd brought it into school to read
at break time. Everyone was still
being quite friendly, but
she hated having to
ask to join in the
games. It was
embarrassing. It
was easier to
sit on one of
the benches
and read.

This week's magazine had a big article on animal charities and an interview with the manager of a Cats Protection League shelter. She was talking about how important it was to find cats new homes quickly, as they didn't really like being kept all together. They wanted a place to call their own. Lucy sighed to herself as she thought of the black-and-white kitten.

But the really strange thing was that the Cats Protection League lady also said that black cats and black-and-white ones were much harder to find homes for than tabbies or gingers. Lucy just couldn't understand why. The article said that people thought black-and-white cats were a bit ordinary, not pretty like tabbies.

It made Lucy so cross that she almost tore the page, she was gripping it so tightly. How could people think that? All cats and kittens were different! Jessie's cat Socks was white, with a ginger tail and a funny ginger stripe down his nose. But that didn't mean he was a better pet than the little black-and-white kitten would be.

The article also said that some people didn't want cats that were black all over because they were worried that they might not be seen on the road and could get run over. At least that made sense, Lucy thought. But they could always get their black cat a reflective collar, couldn't they?

"If I ever get a cat, I'm definitely going to a shelter and choosing a black-

and-white one," she murmured. "Or a lovely black cat. Like a witch's cat."

"Is it good?"

Lucy jumped so hard she nearly banged her head on the back of the bench and the girl leaning over to talk to her gasped.

"Sorry! I didn't mean to scare you. I get that magazine sometimes too. I was just wondering if it was a good one this week."

"Oh!" Lucy nodded and smiled. "Yes. But sort of sad. There's a big bit about shelters. And it says not many people choose the black cats. I was just thinking I definitely would."

"Oh, me too," the other girl agreed.

Lucy thought frantically, trying to remember her name. There were loads of girls in her class, but she thought this one was called Sara. "Our cat's mostly black, but he's got a white front and white paws. My mum says he looks like he's wearing a penguin suit." She leaned over and looked at the article. "What's that about National Black Cat Day?"

Lucy looked at the bubble down near the bottom of the page. She hadn't got there yet. "The Cats Protection League invented it! To show everyone that black cats are special. It's in October – oh, the same day as Halloween. I suppose that makes sense. But black cats aren't all spooky."

Sara giggled. "They're good at appearing out of nowhere, though. I'm always tripping over Harvey."

"Aw, that's such a cute name for a cat." Lucy smiled.

"He just looks like a Harvey," Sara explained. "Even when he was a kitten, there was something Harvey-ish about him. Have you got a cat?" she added, looking at Lucy sideways. There was something hopeful about the way she asked it, as though she wanted someone to share cat stories with. A friend who had a cat of her own – what could be better than that?

It was the first time someone had really seemed interested in her at school. If she said no, Sara would shrug and smile and walk away, Lucy was sure of it. And she was just as sure that she didn't want that to happen. So she nodded, slowly, trying to think about what to say. "Yes. We've got a kitten." She slipped her hand under the magazine and crossed her fingers. She hated to lie, especially to someone as nice as Sara, but she had to. "We've only just got her." It was almost true, wasn't it? She wanted that little black-and-white kitten from the alleyway to be theirs, so much…

"Oh, you're so lucky! Is she gorgeous? What does she look like? How old is she?"

Lucy swallowed. "She's black and white, like Harvey. And she's very little, only just old enough to leave her mother. She was a stray."

"What's she called?" Sara demanded eagerly.

Lucy blinked. She couldn't think. Not a single name would come into her head. What was a good name for a kitten?

Then she smiled at Sara. She knew the perfect name, of course she did.

"She's called Catkin."

Chapter Four

"What's the matter, Lucy?" Gran looked up from her book and peered across the table at her granddaughter's pile of books. "You haven't written anything for ages."

"It's a project." Lucy sighed. "It's difficult. It's about Egyptians and we can make the project about whatever we like – that's what's so hard about it.

I can't choose, even though I've got all these books out of the library."

And, of course, only half her mind was on her project. The rest of it was worrying about having lied to Sara two days ago. Especially as Sara was really, really excited. She kept asking about Catkin, and she obviously really wanted to come and see her. But she was too nice – or maybe too shy – to ask straight out if she could come round. Lucy had a feeling that she was working herself up to it, though.

The awful thing was, Lucy would have liked Sara to come round. She'd love to have a friend home for tea. Gran and Dad kept gently asking if there was anyone she really liked at school and if she wanted to invite somebody over. William had had Harry round and been back to his house too. And he'd been invited to a birthday party already.

But if Sara came round, then she'd know that Lucy had been lying about Catkin and she'd hate her. She might even tell the entire class that Lucy was a liar.

"I went to Egypt, you know," Gran said thoughtfully, breaking into Lucy's thoughts. "It must have been, oh, goodness, eight, ten years ago? Yes, just before you were born, Lucy. We went to see the pyramids, me and one of my old schoolfriends. Auntie Barbara, you remember her?"

Lucy didn't, but she nodded as if she did. "You really went there? What was it like? Did you go and see the Great Pyramid?"

"We certainly did. We went inside it, as well. It was quite frightening," Gran added slowly. "Very shadowy and hard to breathe. I didn't like it much, Lucy, I have to admit, but I'm glad I saw it. And from the outside, they were incredible to look at. Wait a minute." She smiled and got up, walking through into the living room. Lucy could hear her opening drawers in the big display cabinet that had most of her precious, ever-so-breakable ornaments in it.

Gran came back in, carefully unrolling a piece of brownish paper. "Look, this is what I brought back as a souvenir of the holiday, Lucy. It's a papyrus. Like paper but made out of reeds." She held it out. "You can take it, have a look."

Lucy looked at her uncertainly. "Isn't it fragile?" she asked worriedly. She wanted to hold it – she could see that the painting on it was beautiful, a black cat wearing a jewelled necklace and even an earring, it looked like.

"I know you'll be careful." Gran smiled at her. "I ought to get it framed, really, it's such a lovely painting. The box at the side says my name in hieroglyphics. I watched the man doing it."

Lucy took the papyrus, feeling the roughness against her fingers. She could even see the lines of the reed stems in the weave. "The cat's so beautiful," she murmured. Then she grinned up at Gran. "I can't see many cats agreeing to wear all that jewellery, though. Most of them don't even like collars!"

Gran nodded. "But then she's a goddess, this one. Bast, she's called."

Lucy examined the picture again. "There was a cat goddess? Wow... Gran, I could make my project about her!" Very carefully, she laid the papyrus down on the table so she could fling her arms around her gran. "I could copy the painting, maybe. You're so clever!"

As she hugged Gran tightly, Lucy realized something else. Gran couldn't possibly dislike cats that much, could she? Not when she'd chosen a painting of a cat as a special souvenir.

The black-and-white kitten was enjoying a patch of sunlight in the yard. Her mother was off looking for food and the little kitten was stretched out, snoozing, with her nose on her paws.

Her ears fluttered a little as she caught a noise, coming from the back of one of the shops, and then her eyes snapped open. Someone was coming!

She darted back into the safety of the box den, her heart thudding fast against her ribs. The voices were loud, frightening even, and there were heavy feet clumping all around her.

She pressed herself back into the corner of the box, thinking that they would just dump their rubbish in the bins and go. But no one usually came close to the pile of old boxes like this. It wasn't a delivery – no van had driven down the alleyway. She was almost used to *that* noise, although she still didn't like it.

This was something different. And then suddenly the box, her safe, warm box, shifted and split and she let out a high-pitched squeak of fright. What was happening?

"There's something in there," a deep voice growled. "Ugh, not rats?"

"I don't think so – oh, there's a stray cat that hangs around the yard – perhaps it's her?"

Someone clapped their hands loudly, the sound sharp and echoing in the enclosed yard. "Go on, shoo! Off you go, cat!"

The kitten squeaked again and her box tipped sideways. She shot out, terrified, and streaked across the yard, away from the growling voices.

"There she goes – but that's just a kitten. Not much bigger than a rat, poor little thing!"

The kitten huddled in the corner, panicking. Someone was coming towards her, huge boots thumping.

She had never tried to climb the fences before, but anything was better than staying here. She sank her claws in the wood and scrabbled frantically upwards, balancing for a moment on the very top of the fence. Then she jumped down the other side and set off through the bushes, who knew where.

Lucy was stretched out in the long grass, idly picking the blades. She'd done her homework and typed up loads of work for her project on the computer. She felt relaxed and happy in the autumn sun. Gran had given her a sandwich, to keep her going until Dad got home and they could all have dinner together, but Lucy hadn't finished it – she was feeling too lazy even to eat.

She could hear William right down the end of the garden, humming to himself as he investigated the greenhouse. Gran didn't use it very much these days and some of the glass panes were broken, but Dad had told them he'd plant seeds in the springtime. He'd already tidied up the bit of the garden nearest to the house, but Lucy and William loved this wild part, with the overgrown bushes. It was full of hidden nests and little dark caves. Lucy glanced sideways, checking that the big spotted garden spider hanging off the branch by her foot hadn't moved. She didn't mind him being there – he'd probably lived here longer than she had – but she didn't want him getting any closer.

He was still there. But underneath him, peering out at her from the shadows, was a tiny black-and-white face.

A kitten! The same kitten she had seen in the alleyway, Lucy was almost sure. She looked down the garden at the greenhouse and the fence. She hadn't realized before, but the shops were very close to the back of Gran's garden, even though to get to them by the street you had to go quite a way round.

"Did you climb over the fence?" Lucy whispered, very, very quietly.

The kitten stared back at her. She was very small and so thin, Lucy thought. She looked exhausted – as though she was frightened, but too worn out even to run.

Slowly, creeping her fingers across the grass, Lucy stretched out a hand to get her sandwich. It was chicken. Perfect for a kitten treat.

The kitten watched her, wide-eyed, shrinking back a little as Lucy's hand came close. But then she smelled the chicken – Lucy could see the exact moment. Her whiskers twitched and her ears flicked forwards, then her eyes grew even rounder.

Lucy tore off a tiny piece of sandwich and gently laid it down, just where the tufts of long grass met the branches. Then she watched. The kitten didn't have to move far. If she wasn't brave enough, maybe Lucy could throw her a piece further in, but that might scare her away.

The kitten looked at the piece of sandwich and Lucy could see her sniffing. She looked between Lucy and the sandwich a few times, then she wriggled forwards on her stomach, inching slowly towards the food. As soon as she was close enough, she seized the chickeny mouthful and darted back into the safety of the bush.

Lucy wanted to laugh, but she folded her lips together firmly, in case the noise scared the kitten away. She watched the kitten wolf down the scrap and then she tore off a little more.

This time she left it a bit closer to her feet.

The kitten didn't take as long to decide she was going for the food the second time. She gave Lucy one slightly suspicious look and then raced to grab it.

After that, Lucy put the plate down, right next to her feet, to see what would happen. Surely the kitten wouldn't be able to drag away a whole sandwich, would she? She'd have to stop by the plate and eat it there. And then maybe Lucy would be able to stroke her...

The kitten stared at the sandwich. The two pieces she'd already eaten had been so delicious. But now the rest of the sandwich was closer to the girl and she wasn't sure that she was quite brave enough to go and take it.

But the smell... She could taste it in her mouth still and she was really hungry. She hadn't eaten for such a long time. After she had scrambled over the fence the afternoon before, she had run and climbed and run again, frightened and desperate to get away. Her cosy den in the box had suddenly been snatched from her and she didn't understand. She just knew that she wasn't safe there any more.

She had only stopped in the big garden because she was tired. Wriggling through the tiny gap under the back fence had worn her out. She had simply lain down in the dry, shadowy space under the bush and gone to sleep. When she'd woken, it had been dark and she had been so hungry. She'd finally understood that everything was different now. Her mother wasn't there to bring her food and there was no one there to curl up and sleep with. She was lost and all alone.

She had been on her own before, of course she had. But she had always known that her mother would come back. The kitten would purr throatily and her mother would wash her, licking her fur lovingly all over.

Now her fur was dusty and matted with dirt, and a clump of it had torn out when she had squeezed under the fence. She had sat there below the bush and tried to wash herself, but it wasn't the same and it only made her feel more lonely.

The night sounds seemed louder than they'd ever been before. Cars roared past and made her shudder with fright, and people laughed and shouted. Another cat had stalked through the garden, late at night, but it hadn't been her mother. She had jumped up eagerly, ready to run and nuzzle it, but all it had done was stare at her and she'd seen it thicken out its tail. Then it had paced on, away down the side of the house and the kitten had ducked back under the bush, knowing that she was more lost than ever.

As Lucy pursed her lips and tried to make kitten-encouraging noises that sounded something like *prrrrrrp*, the kitten stared back at her and wondered what to do. The girl seemed quiet and gentle, not like those stomping men who had chased her away from her home. And she had food. Just now,

food seemed the most important thing
of all.

Slowly, paw by paw, the kitten
came out of her hiding place and crept
towards Lucy.

Chapter Five

"Lucy…"

"*Shh!*"

"Lucy, is that a kitten? Is that the kitten from by the baker's shop?"

"Yes, but *shh*! Please don't make her run away. She's really shy, William. Look, come and sit down here."

William sat down, as slowly and quietly as he could, and stared at the kitten. She stared back for a moment, but she was so busy devouring the rest of the chicken sandwich that she didn't really have time to worry about him.

"How did she get here?"

"I don't know." Lucy reached out one hand and held it by the plate, close enough for the kitten to sniff. The kitten glared at her and then butted gently at Lucy's hand.

William giggled. "She's telling you to get off her sandwich."

"Maybe. Or she might be putting her scent on me," said Lucy. "That's what a cat's doing when it rubs its face against you. They've got scent glands there. They're saying we belong to them." *I want to belong to you*, she added silently. *Please stay. Please, please, please.*

"Lucy," William whispered. "Do
you think – do you think she could
be our cat? Can we keep her?" He
looked around the garden. "We could
make her a nest in the greenhouse.
Wow, she's actually finished all of that
sandwich. Do you think she wants
another one? Gran asked if I wanted a
sandwich but I said no. I could go and
say that I've changed my mind…"

Lucy looked worried. "I don't like

telling Gran lies – but we can't tell her the truth, can we? Dad said she wouldn't want a pet in the house. And this kitten really needs food. She's so skinny."

"The greenhouse isn't the same as being in the house," William pointed out. "I bet she wouldn't mind. So it doesn't matter if we don't tell her."

Lucy couldn't help thinking that it *did* matter, and that they were just twisting things around to be the way they wanted – but she wouldn't be able to bear it if Gran made them take the kitten back to the alleyway. The greenhouse would be like a palace to a kitten who was used to living in a box. And Gran didn't usually go down to the end of the garden. It would be all right.

And if she really had a kitten, she wouldn't be lying to Sara any more.

"Yes." She nodded. "Go and ask Gran if you can have a sandwich. With lots of chicken."

"Oh dear, what's the matter with that poor little girl?" Gran speeded up as they made their way home from school. She hurried down the pavement towards a toddler, standing outside the baker's shop next to a little scooter and howling. "I hope she's not lost."

"She isn't, Gran, look, I can see her mum coming." Lucy pointed to a lady running towards the little girl.

"Good." Gran bent over the little

girl. "What happened, sweetheart? Did you fall off your scooter?"

The little girl stared back at her and shook her head. She stopped crying.

Gran smiled at the little girl's mother, who had reached them at last and was now crouched next to her daughter, hugging her and all out of breath. "I'm sorry, we didn't see what happened, but she says she didn't fall."

"Mummy! The cat!" And the little girl began to howl again.

"Oh, Macey! Did you try and stroke a cat? Did he scratch you?"

The little girl nodded and wailed louder, holding up her arm towards her mum.

Lucy sucked in her breath through her teeth – Macey had a long scratch down the inside of her arm. It wasn't bleeding very much, but it obviously hurt.

"Some cats are just grumpy, Macey. You know I said not to chase after them." Her mum sighed. "Don't worry, baby. We'll go home and put one of your teddy-bear plasters on it."

Lucy bit her lip. It probably wasn't the right time to say that the cat must have been scared if the little girl had tried to grab it.

"It was probably that stray tabby that lives down the end of the alleyway," Gran said. "Stray cats can be very wild and fierce."

Lucy and William exchanged glances, thinking of the little black-and-white kitten, curled up in the greenhouse back at home. They'd made her a cosy nest out of one of the cardboard boxes they'd had for packing up their things, tipped on its side and lined with an old sweatshirt of Lucy's. Then they'd laid the kitten a trail of chicken sandwich pieces to show her where the greenhouse was.

Lucy and William had done their best to make it into the nicest den a kitten could have. They'd even made her a litter tray, out of an old seed tray they'd found on one of the greenhouse shelves – it had been full of dusty earth. Lucy had a feeling the kitten might not know what it was for, as she was a stray and used to weeing anywhere, but if she was going to be an indoor cat one day, it was important to try. William had brought her a plant saucer full of water from the outside tap, as well.

That morning, before they went to school, Lucy had nipped out with some Weetabix and milk. It wasn't the best thing for a kitten, she knew, but they didn't have any proper cat food. Anyway, the kitten hadn't seemed to mind. She had buried her face in it eagerly and when Lucy finally had to go, the kitten had been blissfully licking milky gunge off her whiskers.

She hadn't looked very wild and
fierce at all. She was still shy, of course.
But when Lucy had arrived with the
bowl, she hadn't run away, or hidden
herself behind the wobbly towers of
flowerpots. Instead, she'd just pricked
her ears, wary, but hopeful.

Lucy and William lagged behind
Gran for the rest of the way home.
"Did you hear what Gran said about
stray cats being fierce?" William asked
anxiously.

Lucy nodded. "I know. I was really wishing we could tell her about Catkin."

"Catkin?" William blinked in surprise. "You named her?" He frowned a little. Lucy could tell he was hurt that she'd given the kitten a name without talking to him.

"Gran used to have a black-and-white cat called Catkin," Lucy explained. "She was telling me about her. It's a really sweet name and I thought that maybe if we called the kitten Catkin too, it would remind her of it. But now Gran's thinking about nasty fierce cats instead. It's the worst timing ever."

"Ohhh." William nodded. "I see. But our Catkin's sweet, Lucy. She's not fierce at all. Gran will see that, won't she?"

"Mmmm. But let's not tell her just yet that we've got Catkin in the greenhouse. She'll have to go on being our secret kitten. And don't tell Dad, either!"

"Come on, you two!" Gran called back. "It's starting to rain."

Lucy and William sped up, the first fat drops splashing on to the pavement as they dashed after Gran.

"What if she gets wet?" William hissed. "The greenhouse has got all those big holes in the roof! She'll get wet!"

"You're right," Lucy muttered back. She smiled at William. "You know that big old wardrobe in my bedroom… Perhaps we could hide her in there?"

"Why not my bedroom?" William said.

"Because you haven't got a wardrobe, just drawers. And because your bedroom's next to Dad's! Mine's up those creaky stairs and I can always hear people coming. So I've got time to hide a kitten in my wardrobe before they get to the top, you see?"

"I suppose so." William sighed heavily.

Lucy smiled to herself, imagining falling asleep tonight with the faint sound of purring echoing out from her wardrobe. Or maybe even a small furry ball of kitten on the end of her bed. "I hope she understands we're trying to help," Lucy said suddenly. "She might not want to come inside.

She's probably never been in a house before." Lucy had thought they'd be able to tempt Catkin inside gradually. She'd never thought of doing it so soon.

William grinned at her. "I think if you gave her a chicken sandwich she'd probably go anywhere!"

Chapter Six

"Distract Gran! Show her your cut knee," Lucy muttered, thinking of Macey and her scratch. She had the wet kitten and her old sweatshirt bundled up in her arms and there was a lot of squeaking and wriggling going on. She'd taken the cold sausages from her lunch box (she'd saved them on purpose) and they'd nipped outside while Gran was taking off her coat and changing into her slippers. Catkin had been so excited about the sausages, she'd hardly minded when Lucy had picked her up. But now Lucy needed a clear run upstairs. "Go in the utility room… Pretend you're looking for the first-aid box. Quick!" The armful of sweatshirt was wriggling like mad. "It's all right, Catkin. Just a tiny bit longer."

William nipped in through the back door and then into the utility room. If he could get Gran to follow him in there, she wouldn't see Lucy dash past.

"Gran! My knee's bleeding! Can you get me a plaster? I fell over at school."

Lucy could hear Gran bustling through the kitchen and then the squeak of the utility-room door. It was on Dad's DIY list to oil that door, so she was glad he hadn't done it yet. Huddling Catkin close, she darted through the kitchen, into the hallway and up the stairs.

In her room, she kicked the door gently shut and put her bundle down on the floor. Catkin shook her way out of the sweatshirt looking indignant and hissed faintly at Lucy.

"Sorry," Lucy whispered back. "I couldn't let Gran see you. And it's really pouring with rain out there now. I bet your box is soggy already. I'll make you a new bed, look."

She grabbed another cardboard box off the teetering pile in the corner of her room and put it sideways in the bottom of her wardrobe, shoving all her shoes to one side. Catkin was still standing on the sweatshirt, so Lucy made a nest shape out of her woolly winter scarf and put that in the box instead. Then she put the last half of sausage down in front of the box too. It was still sitting in one of Gran's neat little plastic lunch pots, which made a perfect cat-food bowl.

"I'll get you some water in a minute," Lucy promised. "And the litter tray. Your things are just outside the back door. William brought them in from the greenhouse."

She looked at her kitten home thoughtfully and then at Catkin, who had slunk under her bed. The kitten looked worried.

"I know it's strange," Lucy told her quietly. "But we're nice. Really. And there's more sausage, look." She tapped her fingernails against the wardrobe door to make Catkin look and then tipped up the lunch pot to show her. "Did you want another chicken sandwich instead? Are they your favourite? They're my favourite too."

Catkin edged out from under the bed, sniffing. She was confused. But she had never had so much food before – her brother and sister had always fought for more of their mother's milk and the same with the scraps. It wasn't just the sandwiches and the cereal or the sausages, either – the two children had been so gentle. Lucy and William had whispered to her and tried to purr at her and that morning Lucy had run one finger softly all down her back, which had made her quiver. It had been strange and different, but she had liked it. And now there was another soft box bed and more food. She liked being inside, all warm and dry. So she padded cautiously across the room and stopped to sniff at Lucy's fingers. Then she butted her head up against Lucy's hand and went to nibble daintily at the sausage in the pot.

Lucy sat watching her, smiling to herself. Her own kitten. In her own bedroom. Almost, anyway.

Then she froze. The steps up to her room were creaking. She was just sitting forwards, ready to scoop Catkin further into the wardrobe and close the door, when she heard William hissing, "It's only me! I've got the tray!"

Lucy wriggled back slowly and went to open the door. "You star! How did you do that?"

"Gran's on the phone to Auntie Susie. She'll be ages. Angel Katie got a distinction in her ballet exam." Angel Katie was what they called their perfect little cousin. "Gran was in the living room and she didn't see me at all. I've got the water too."

"That's brilliant. Look, if I move my shoes and put them under my desk instead, we can put the litter tray in the corner of the wardrobe. And this newspaper I used to wrap my photo frames can go underneath, just in case. Don't worry, Catkin. We're just making it nice for you."

"I hope she understands what to do," William said doubtfully. "What if she wees in the wrong place? Like, I don't know, in your slippers?"

Lucy grinned at him. "Yuck. But actually, I don't think I'd mind. She's only little. I remember when you were a baby and you weed in Dad's face when he was changing your nappy."

William went scarlet. "You don't! You can't remember that, you were only little yourself."

"Well, I remember Dad telling me about it once, anyway. I bet Catkin won't make as much mess as a baby."

Catkin finished the sausage and sniffed thoughtfully at the litter tray. Then she snuggled up on Lucy's scarf and pulled the sweater over herself, almost like a blanket. She tucked her nose comfortably under her tail and, as the two children watched, she fell fast asleep.

"I hope Gran didn't go into your room for anything today," William whispered to Lucy, as they hurried across the playground the next afternoon. It was Friday and everyone was running and swinging their bags, eager to get home and start the weekend.

"Me too. But I don't think she would have done. I took all of my washing downstairs and put it in the machine for her. And Dad vacuumed my room a couple of days ago. Catkin was really good last night. She didn't mew or anything and she even used the litter tray. This morning she was sitting on my windowsill when I woke up, just looking out of the window."

Lucy crossed her fingers. "Look, there's Gran by the gate. She doesn't look cross, does she? Not like someone who's found a kitten in a wardrobe." They waved to Gran and she waved back, smiling.

Just then someone called out her name, "Lucy!" It was Sara.

Lucy swung round and beamed at her friend. "Hello!"

"Lucy, can I ask you a big favour?" Sara said pleadingly, as they walked towards the gate. "I live quite close to you, you know. Just a couple of streets further on. Do you think I could pop into your house for five minutes on the way home? Just to see your gorgeous kitten? Pleeease? My mum said it was fine if you said I could."

Lucy stopped walking and swallowed hard. She so wanted to say yes. Perhaps she could even tell Sara the secret. But there wasn't time. Gran would hear them, she was really close. In fact, she was coming towards them, smiling. She was probably about to invite Sara to come for tea.

"I-I can't today…" Lucy whispered, her eyes darting sideways at Gran. "I've got – dancing." Gran had been talking about signing her up for dance classes – there were some at the church hall, not far away. It was the first thing that came into her head.

It was just a pity that William blurted out, "I've got to go to football!" at the same time.

"We've got both," Lucy said

hurriedly. "It's just not a good day,
Friday."

Gran was standing beside them now,
looking curious, and Lucy could see
Sara's mum coming over too.

"If you don't want me to come—"
Sara started to say, sounding a bit hurt.

"It isn't that! I do want you to,
I really do!"

"You just had
to say no – I
thought we
were friends!"

"We are!"
Lucy said
anxiously.
"It's just –
not today.
Another day!"

Sara nodded, but she still looked really disappointed. She grabbed her mum's hand and pulled her away down the street, leaving Lucy and William and Gran staring at each other in confusion.

"Lucy, whatever's the matter? Wasn't that Sara, that nice girl who lives on Foxglove Way? Have you fallen out with her?"

"Yes." Lucy sniffed. "She wanted to come to our house."

"Well, why didn't you let her? She could have had dinner with us."

"It wasn't that. I can't explain. Please can we go home?" Lucy reached out and took Gran's hand. "Please."

"All right." But Gran still sounded worried and she kept hold of Lucy's hand as they walked on. Lucy could tell she hadn't finished asking about what had happened. "Lucy, was Sara asking about a kitten?" she said at last, as they walked past the alleyway. "I thought I heard her say something about visiting a kitten…"

Lucy swallowed. "But we haven't got a kitten," she pointed out, trying to sound cheerful.

"Lucy…" Gran pulled her hand gently to make her stop. "Just go on ahead for a minute, William. Look, you can take my keys. Go and open the front door. We'll follow you." She watched as William walked on ahead and then she followed, walking along slowly with Lucy's hand held tight in hers. "Lucy, did you tell Sara you had a kitten?"

Lucy didn't say anything. How could she explain?

Gran went on thoughtfully. "Sometimes it's hard, when you really want to make friends – you make up stories. Little stories to make yourself sound more interesting. Everyone does it sometimes, Lucy, it's all right."

Lucy gaped up at her. "How did you know?"

"Like I said, everyone does it. But almost everyone gets found out too, Lucy love. You're going to have to explain to Sara and say you're sorry, you know."

Lucy kicked at the pavement with her foot. "I know," she muttered. But inside she was saying, *I didn't make*

*it up. It wasn't a lie. Well, it was when
I first said it. But now I'm lying to you
instead... I wish we'd told you about
Catkin in the first place. What am I
going to do?*

"Are you that desperate for a
kitten?" Gran asked suddenly.

Lucy blinked, shocked out of her
worries. "Um. I would love one. But
Dad said you didn't like pets. Because
they were dirty."

Gran sniffed. "Well, I do like
everything to be clean," she agreed.
"But a little cat... Maybe we could
think about it."

Lucy swallowed hard and tried to
smile. Somehow she had to explain
to Gran that they had a little cat
already...

When they got back to the house, Gran made hot chocolate and she even put marshmallows on the top, as a treat. She let Lucy and William take it upstairs, though she did say they had to be careful not to spill any.

"Dinner will be in about an hour," she reminded them. "Your dad's working late tonight, so we're not waiting for him today."

Lucy and William carried the hot chocolate upstairs to Lucy's room, with the sandwiches they'd both saved from lunch. At the top of the steps, outside the door, they stopped and looked at each other worriedly. Somehow Lucy felt convinced that the kitten wouldn't be there. Perhaps they had imagined it all. She reached out and turned the handle, peering cautiously around the door.

Over in the wardrobe, the kitten lifted her head and yawned. Then she looked up at them and nosed at the empty plastic pot, clearly hoping for some tea.

"Hello," Lucy whispered, starting to shred up her sandwich. "Did you miss us?"

Catkin yawned again and, very faintly, Lucy heard her purr.

"You're pleased to see us! You're actually purring. Oh, Catkin. If only we could show you to Gran right now, I'm sure she'd want to keep you." She patted Catkin's head, loving the feeling of the silky fur under her fingers. "This weekend, somehow, we'll find a way to tell her. We have to."

Chapter Seven

When Lucy and William's dad got home late that night, he sat across the kitchen table from their gran, eating his dinner.

"What's the matter?" he asked, as he wiped a bit of bread round his plate to mop up the gravy. "You've hardly said anything since I got home, Mum."

Gran sighed and put down her mug

of tea. "I'm just a bit worried about Lucy. I'm not sure she's settling all that well with the other girls at school. She had a bit of an argument with one of them this afternoon, just as I was picking her up. She didn't want to talk about it very much, but it seems as though she'd told this girl – Sara, her name is – that we had a kitten."

Dad stared at her. "But why on earth would she say that?"

Gran shrugged. "To fit in? To make herself a bit more exciting? We're asking a lot of them, you know, starting at a new school."

Dad's shoulders slumped. "I suppose so. But I thought it was the best thing to do…"

"I still think it is." Gran reached over and patted his hand. "But I'm wondering if a pet would help Lucy settle."

"You don't like pets!"

"Whatever gave you that idea? I wouldn't want a dog, I couldn't manage the walking, but I love cats!" Gran smiled at him, a little sadly. "Actually, I suppose we didn't have any pets when you were younger, did we? I haven't had a cat of my own for a long time. Not since Catkin died. He was twenty, you know,

and I'd had him since I was a little girl.
I didn't want another cat for a while
after that and somehow then it just
never seemed to be the right time. But I
wouldn't mind a cat now. Especially with
Lucy and Wiliam to help look after it."

"Well, it would be wonderful for
Lucy," Dad agreed. "I always said no
before, because we were out of the house
all the time." He got up and took his
plate over to the dishwasher. "I'll go and
check on her. I know she'll probably be
asleep, but I just want to see that she's all
right…"

Catkin woke up as the morning light
shone into Lucy's room. She didn't have

any blinds yet and the morning was bright and sunny. The kitten stretched blissfully, padding her paws into a patch of sun just outside the wardrobe. Then she hunched up the other way, arching her back like a spitting witch's cat and stepped delicately out into Lucy's bedroom.

Lucy was still fast asleep, huddled up under her duvet, so Catkin jumped up on to the bed to sniff at her. She smelled interesting, like breakfast and warm sunshine. But she didn't wake up when Catkin dabbed a chilly nose against her ear – only muttered and turned over, which made the duvet shift alarmingly. Catkin sprang down before she slid off and sat on the rug.

When she'd washed her ears
thoroughly, both sides, she stalked
off across the room. Something was
different and she hadn't quite worked
out what it was. There was something
in the air, something fresh and new.

The door was open!

Lucy had shut it carefully, of course,
when she came upstairs to bed. But

then her dad had come up to check on her. Catkin and Lucy had both been fast asleep and neither of them had seen that he had left the door ajar. Just wide enough for a small, determined paw to hook it open.

Catkin nosed her way out and started to hop carefully – front feet, then back feet – down the stairs. It felt unfamiliar. Then she trotted along the landing, sniffing curiously at the different doors. She padded into William's room, but a wobbly pile of books slid over when she nudged it, so she darted out again and set off down the next flight of stairs to the bottom. She sniffed her way carefully down the hallway and into the kitchen.

Most of the food was shut away in cupboards, but Dad had left a loaf of bread out on the counter and Catkin could smell it. She sat on the floor, staring up and thinking...

Lucy woke up when the sunny patch from the window moved round on to her bed. She blinked sleepily, wondering why it was that she felt so happy and scared all at the same time. Then she sat up straight, remembering.

Catkin!

Today they *had* to find a way to tell Gran and Dad what had happened, and make them see that Catkin needed to stay with them.

The kitten wasn't sitting on the windowsill the way she had been the day before, so Lucy kneeled up in bed and leaned over to peer into the wardrobe. "Catkin," she called. "Puss, puss, puss…"

But no little kitten face appeared and Lucy's heart began to beat faster. "Where did you go?" she murmured. She hopped out of bed and crouched down to check underneath, but there was nothing there except dust. No Catkin hiding in the cardboard boxes, or behind the little bookshelf by the door.

The open door.

Lucy gasped. "I shut it!" she whispered to herself. "I know I did. Oh no." She hurried down the stairs,

going as fast as she could on tiptoe,
so as not to wake Dad or Gran. She
dashed into William's room.

"Wake up! William, wake up! Have
you seen Catkin? I don't know where
she is."

William stared at her sleepily,
blinking like an owl, and then he
squeaked and jumped out of bed.

"Where would she go?"

"Shh! I don't know, maybe the kitchen?"

William nodded. "Definitely the kitchen."

They hurried down the stairs, freezing to a stop every time one of them creaked. The house was old and they hadn't had time to learn which stairs to step over.

"Dad'll hear us," Lucy whispered miserably. "Hurry up, we have to find her and get her back into my room." She kneeled down on the kitchen floor, looking around. She hadn't noticed how many tiny, kitten-sized hiding places there were in here before. On the chairs, under the table. Down the side of the oven. "Oh! What if she's climbed into the washing machine?" Lucy gasped. "I read about a cat who did that once."

But the washing machine was empty and so were all the other spots they could think of. Lucy sat down on the floor, looking helpless. "I can't think of anywhere else," she murmured. "All the windows are closed, aren't they?"

William nodded. "It was cold last night. Unless – Gran always sleeps with her bedroom window open."

A large tear spilled down the side of Lucy's nose. "Maybe she went out that way, then. She didn't want to stay. Catkin's gone!"

Chapter Eight

"Whatever's the matter with you two? Why are you up at seven o'clock on a Saturday morning?" Gran demanded. She was standing in the kitchen doorway, wrapped in her dressing gown. "Lucy, you're crying! What's wrong?" She put her arms around Lucy, pulling her up from the floor.

"We've lost her!" Lucy sobbed into

Gran's shoulder. She didn't care about keeping Catkin a secret any more. It was too late now.

"Lost who?" Gran stared at Lucy in puzzlement and so did Dad, who'd come in behind her, looking sleepy.

"Catkin," William explained, coming to lean against Dad's dressing gown. "Our kitten. Lucy found her in the garden. She was in Lucy's wardrobe, but when we woke up she'd gone."

"You had a kitten shut in your wardrobe?" Dad said slowly.

"Not shut in," Lucy shook her head, gulping back tears. "Just her bed was in there and her litter tray. She could go anywhere in my room. We couldn't leave her in the greenhouse – the glass is full of holes and it was pouring with rain on Thursday night."

Dad and Gran looked shocked. "But what were you feeding her?" Gran asked, frowning.

"Sandwiches, mostly. She loves chicken." Lucy sniffed. "Just like me. We saved bits of our lunches for her and she was getting tame. We thought she was going to stay with us, but now she's run away. She must have gone through your window, Gran. It's the only one that was open." Lucy slumped down on one of the kitchen chairs.

Gran moved slowly over to the counter to put the kettle on, tidying away the breadcrumbs and pushing shut a half-open drawer on the way. "I need a cup of tea," she murmured. "A kitten in your wardrobe…"

"Where did she come from in the first place? That's what I want to know," Dad said, sitting down opposite Lucy with William on his knee.

"The alley down by the baker's," Lucy explained tiredly. "There were three of them – the two tabbies got adopted, but nobody cared about the little black-and-white kitten. And then she just turned up in our garden."

"And you named her Catkin? Like my Catkin?" Gran asked, getting mugs out of the cupboard.

"You said your kitten was black and white too," Lucy explained. "And it's a sweet name. It was just right."

"Oh dear," Gran sighed. "Perhaps she was just too wild to be a pet, Lucy. If she's never really known people…"

"But she wasn't wild," Lucy tried to explain. She could feel herself starting to cry again. "She was shy, but she purred at us. And she loved our food, even if she didn't really love us yet."

"Well, perhaps we could go back to the alley by the shops and look for her," Gran said thoughtfully, leaning over to get a clean tea towel out of the drawer.

"You mean – if we found her we could bring her back home again?" Lucy gasped. "We can keep her?" She jumped up. "Can we go round there now?"

William wriggled off Dad's knee. "Right now?"

But Gran was standing staring into the tea-towel drawer. "I don't think we need to… Look."

Lucy leaned over and clapped her hand across her mouth. Curled up in among Gran's neatly ironed tea towels was a black-and-white kitten, half-asleep and blinking up at them in confusion.

"I shut the drawer…" Gran murmured.

"When I went to make the tea. It was open, just a little. You know how that drawer sticks sometimes…"

"Just enough for a skinny kitten to climb in, but not enough for us to see her!" Lucy said, her eyes wide.

Sleepily, Catkin stared up at Lucy and Gran and let out a little purr. Perhaps there was going to be food. The bread seemed a long while ago and it had been a lot of effort to get up on to the counter and steal a slice. She was hungry again.

"What a sweetheart," Gran said, laughing as Catkin stepped carefully out of her nest in the drawer. She rubbed her furry face against Gran's hand and purred even louder. "Just like my Catkin," Gran said, petting her ears. "You're staying now, are you?"

Catkin jumped down to the floor and wove her way round Gran's ankles and then Lucy's, still purring.

"That means yes," Lucy whispered. "I know it does."

"You actually had her hidden in your wardrobe?" Sara asked Lucy again, as they followed Gran home from school on Monday afternoon. "You had a secret kitten?"

"Yes. And I really wanted you to see her, but I couldn't let Gran find out. Or I thought I couldn't. It turns out we probably should have just told her to start with."

"That wouldn't have been as exciting," Sara said, shaking her head.

"No." Lucy smiled at her. "It *was* lovely, Catkin being our secret. But now we can play with her without worrying about Dad and Gran. And she still likes my bedroom best in all of the house."

"Shall we pop in and buy a cake for after tea, girls?" Gran suggested, stopping as they reached the baker's. "Oh, William, come back!"

Lucy and Sara giggled as William raced ahead, flinging open the door of the baker's. When they caught up with him, he was already telling Emma behind the counter that he wanted a marshmallow ice cream.

"You know the black-and-white

kitten, the one that was living in your yard?" Lucy said shyly to Emma, after they'd chosen their cakes. "She came into our garden and we're going to keep her!"

Emma smiled delightedly. "Oh, that's such good news! I looked for her, after you two told me she was there, but I never saw her. I did wonder if you'd imagined her."

"No, she's just a bit shy." Lucy smiled to herself, remembering Catkin chasing madly round the kitchen after a ping-pong ball that morning and then collapsing in her lap, exhausted, with her paws in the air. She wasn't shy with them, not any more.

"I've got news for you too," Emma went on, as she put their chocolate doughnuts into a bag. "I called the cat shelter about the kittens' mum, to ask them what the best thing was to do. They're going to catch her and spay her so she doesn't have more kittens. They said she probably won't ever be tame enough to be a house cat, but if she's not trying to feed kittens all the time she'll be a lot less thin and worried, poor thing. So they'll bring her back and she can live in the yard. We'll put scraps out for her."

"Thank you!" Lucy forgot to be shy and gave Emma a hug. "You're amazing. I never even thought of doing that!"

"Maybe Catkin can come back and visit her," William suggested, reaching into his bag and picking the hundreds and thousands off his marshmallow ice cream.

"Maybe." Lucy smiled, imagining the two cats nose to nose, sniffing hello. All of a sudden she couldn't wait to get home and see Catkin and show her off to Sara too.

Her own kitten, not-so-secret any more…

The Brave Kitten

For Helena and her beautiful cat Karmel, whose story I borrowed for this book

Chapter One

"We'd better hurry, Helena," Lucy said, glancing at her watch and walking faster. "There's loads to do this morning, with two dogs coming in to be operated on. I need to get everything ready."

"I'll help," Helena said cheerfully, twirling along the pavement in front of her cousin. Helping out at the surgery was her biggest treat. "I can do the feeding and clean the cages on my own. I know what I'm doing."

Lucy grinned at her. "I know you do. You're like the youngest veterinary nurse in the country, Helena – you've had almost as much practice as me."

"I haven't decided yet what I want to be – whether I should be a nurse or an actual vet," Helena said seriously. "Being a vet's harder. And I'm not sure about doing operations. I don't really like blood. But maybe I'd get used to it."

"You do," Lucy said. "I didn't like it much when I first started training as a nurse, but now it doesn't bother me at all."

"I suppose that cute lop-eared rabbit has already gone home?" Helena asked. She'd loved stroking the rabbit when

she'd gone to see Lucy at the surgery
after school a couple of days before.
"He was so friendly and— Lucy, what's
that?" Helena stopped dancing along
the pavement and peered worriedly
at the parked car up ahead of them.
There was a little mound of pale, sandy
fur tucked just underneath the car.

"Oh no…" Lucy murmured. "Helena,
don't look, OK? Just wait there."

"What is it?" Helena asked. She was suddenly feeling a little bit sick and her heart was jumping. She didn't want to go closer and see whatever it was. But at the same time she couldn't just stay back. The little heap of fur looked like a cat to her, but cats didn't usually lie sprawled like that, not on a road, anyway. Only if they were somewhere warm and safe. "Is it a cat?" she whispered miserably to Lucy, coming closer. "Has it been run over?"

Lucy glanced back at her, frowning, but she could see that Helena wasn't going to stay out of the way. Her cousin loved cats, even though she didn't have one of her own. And Lucy knew how sensible she was. "I think so. Don't cry, Helena. It must have been quick."

But Helena wasn't listening. "Lucy, look! He moved! I'm sure he did."

Lucy whipped round. The little cat had been so cold and lifeless that she hadn't thought he could still be alive, but Helena was right. He'd twitched, just a bit. "Oh, wow…" she muttered. "We need to get him to the surgery, now. Molly and Pete should be in soon – he's definitely going to need a vet to look at him."

"How are we going to get him there, though? Won't it hurt him if we pick him up?" Helena crouched down by the car, peering at the little cat. One of his back legs was really swollen and seemed to be at a funny angle, and she could hardly see him breathing at all. But his eyes were open now, just a tiny slit of gold. He was looking at them.

"Yes," Lucy admitted. "And he might not want us to touch him, either. But we need to get him there quickly. He's in shock, and I've got a feeling he's been here for ages – he's so cold." She pulled off her big scarf and gently wrapped it round the cat, scooping him up and trying to support the injured leg as well as she could.

Helena watched, biting her lip. She'd seen cats at the surgery hissing and scratching at Lucy and the vets because they were frightened or hurting. She hoped this cat wasn't going to fight – he didn't look as though he had the strength.

Maybe he was just too weak, or maybe he understood that Lucy and Helena were trying to help, but the cat lay still in Lucy's arms as they hurried down the street. Helena was jogging beside Lucy, carrying her bag and looking up at the cat. His head was drooping over Lucy's arm, and from time to time his mouth opened in a tiny, soundless mew.

"You might be hurting him," Helena told Lucy worriedly.

"I know. But we're nearly there. Look, I can see Molly's car, she's arrived already."

Helena pushed open the surgery door and looked around. Molly must be out the back somewhere, or upstairs making a coffee.

"Helena, you hold him." Lucy carefully passed over the scarf-wrapped bundle. "Take him into the back room. I'll go and find Molly."

Helena stood there helplessly. The cat hardly weighed anything at all and he wasn't moving. She had an awful feeling he wasn't going to survive – he was too weak. "Just hold on," she whispered, as she carried him through to the room where Molly and Pete operated. She wondered if she ought to put him down on the table, but she didn't want to. The table was cold and hard, and she wanted the cat to know that somebody loved him. "Just hold on, *please*... We're going to make you better."

The golden cat opened his eyes and gazed up at her. He didn't understand what was going on. Everything seemed to hurt and he was frightened. He still wasn't sure what had happened – there had been bright lights suddenly flashing out of the darkness and so much noise. He didn't remember anything after that, until he had woken up at the side of the road and his legs wouldn't work properly.

He had wanted so much to go home, to curl up in his basket, and hide away until he felt better. But he was so dizzy and sick, he wasn't really sure where home was. And it hurt to move. He couldn't walk, one of his back legs wasn't working at all and the other one ached. He could only do a strange sort of hop, dragging his bad leg behind him. He'd managed to get a little way up the road, but then he'd felt so cold and weary, he'd hidden under the parked car. Once he'd lain down, it just seemed too hard to get up again.

Now he could feel the warmth of the girl's arms round him. He liked the softness of her voice too. She sounded gentle and he rubbed his head against her arm, just a little, to show her he was grateful. But it hurt too much to do anything more and his eyes flickered closed again.

"Lucy, he woke up a bit, but now I think he's getting worse!" Helena said anxiously, as Lucy and Molly clattered down the stairs and into the operating room. "He's gone really limp. Please say you can help him, Molly, he's such a sweet cat. He hasn't hissed or scratched or anything."

Molly took the cat and laid him carefully on the table. "Definitely a broken leg," she murmured. "But it's the shock that's really dangerous at the moment. Let's get him on a drip. That'll get some fluids back into him," she explained, seeing Helena frown. "It's a bit like you having one of those energy drinks after you've been running."

"Oh." Helena nodded, wishing the cat would open his eyes again. He looked so weak. He hadn't even flinched when Molly had moved him.

"Once he's warmed through we can examine him properly," Molly explained. "I don't want to fuss him with X-rays while he's like this. But we can at least check if he's got a microchip, so that if he has, we can ring his owner."

Lucy passed her the microchip scanner and Molly held it above the cat's neck – but it didn't beep. It didn't make any sound at all.

"No chip," Molly sighed. "Oh well. We can put a sign up in the surgery window, I suppose."

"But what if his owners never find out where he is?" Helena asked, her voice shaking a little. Life seemed so hard for the poor cat – run over and now maybe homeless as well.

"Once they realize he's missing, I'm sure they'll ring round the local vets," Lucy told her comfortingly. But she glanced at Molly. "Are we going to be OK to operate?" she asked. "I mean, he is very skinny. If he's a stray..."

Molly nodded, frowning. "I know. We could send him over to the PDSA clinic – they'd treat him. But he's so wobbly already, I don't think it's a good idea to move him."

"Why can't you sort his leg out here?" Helena asked. She didn't understand what was going on. Surely they needed to operate on the cat as soon as they could? Helena knew that Molly sometimes worked as a volunteer vet at the PDSA clinic, which was for pets whose owners had problems paying for expensive vet treatments. But why did the cat have to go there?

Lucy put an arm round her shoulders. "It depends on the X-ray, but he might need to have the broken leg pinned," she explained. "It's a really expensive operation and then he's going to need to be looked after for a while. Plus he'll have to have another operation to take the pins out. If he's a stray, there's no one to pay for all that, or for his medicine."

"And even if he does have an owner, they might not be able to afford the treatment." Molly ran her hand over the cat's caramel-coloured ears, looking sad.

"You mean, you might not be able to

do the operation?" Helena whispered. "Even if it would make him better?"

"Of course we want to sort him out," Molly explained. "He's young enough to recover really well. But…"

"You have to!" Helena's eyes filled with tears as she stroked the cat under the chin. "He's so lovely. He nuzzled me… He's trusting us to look after him!"

"I bet the PDSA would help look after him while he's getting better," Molly said, eyeing the cat thoughtfully. "They might cover the costs if we have to operate too." She crouched down to be eye to eye with the caramel cat and gave a firm little nod. "We have to help him."

Chapter Two

The caramel-coloured cat lay in his
cage, staring out at the dimly lit
room. He didn't understand where he
was or what was happening. He was
dazed and he felt sick. And there was
still something wrong with his leg. It
felt worse, if anything. It was aching
and heavy, and he couldn't move
it properly. It smelled wrong too –

strange and sharp with chemicals. He hated it. Wearily, he pulled himself up on his front legs so he could look at his leg properly. It was that weird white wrapping all over his leg that smelled odd.

He leaned over, wincing as the weight pressed on to the broken leg, and pulled at the bandage that lined the cast with his teeth. If he could just get that off, then his leg would be all right again, he was certain...

"I wasn't sure you'd be up yet!" said Lucy, smiling at Helena, who was standing outside her front door with her coat on, looking impatient.

"Mum's still got her pyjamas on," Helena admitted, pointing over her shoulder, and Lucy spotted her aunt waving at her out of the kitchen window. "I know it's early, but I really want to see how the cat is."

"I'm sure he'll be fine," Lucy said. "Molly stayed overnight, remember. One of the vets always does when there's a serious case and she was worried about him. There's a bed upstairs and she'll have popped down every couple of hours to check on him. Bye, Auntie Clare!" she called to Helena's mum. "I'll drop her off in time for lunch – I'm only going in to help Molly out this morning. I hope she's managed to get some sleep," Lucy added to Helena. "That bed's really lumpy. We'll go and make her a cup of tea and some toast."

But when they got to the surgery, Molly was already up, and she looked upset when she opened the front door to them.

"What's wrong?" Lucy asked.

"I don't know how he did it." Molly shook her head frustratedly. "I only checked on him a couple of hours ago and he was still dozing. He looked fine. But I've just been in and he's pulled the cast off." She sighed. "We went with a cast because it was a fairly simple break, but at this rate he's going to make it worse."

"Can you put another cast on?" Helena asked, as they followed Molly to the ward.

"We'll have to. But the more he messes around with that leg, the longer it's going to take to heal. We'll just have to keep an eye on him. He'll probably need a cone collar on now to stop him trying to tug the cast off, but he'll hate it and he's pretty miserable already. This time I'm going to use a special sort of cast that tastes horrible if cats try and chew it, so I'm hoping he'll just leave it alone."

"Poor little cat," Helena said, looking into the small cage where the kitten was stretched out on a blanket. He looked back at her wearily and she could see how sad he was. He was squashed right into the corner of the cage, as if he was trying to hide from everyone. "I bet he hates being shut up in here."

"He needs to be kept still, though," Lucy explained. "Even if he went home, he'd have to stay in a small room – maybe even a dog crate or something – to stop him doing something silly."

"Has anyone phoned about him?" Helena asked Molly hopefully. "His owners?"

Molly shook her head. "No, no one's called. I'd better put up a notice."

"I could make some on the computer," Helena suggested. "We could print them out and put them up close to where we found him too. His owners must be really worried about him." She shivered, thinking about how lovely it would be to have a cat of her very own, and how frightened she'd feel if he simply disappeared.

"Posters would be good." Molly nodded. "OK. Plaster cast number two..."

"Please don't try and pull this one off," Helena murmured to the cat. He was back in his cage with the new cast on, and she'd brought him some food and water. "And don't put your foot in the water bowl, either. When I broke my arm, I wasn't allowed to get it wet at all."

She crouched down on the floor in front of the cage. There were six of them, in two rows on top of each other, and the caramel cat was in one of the bottom ones. "You look really miserable," Helena told him. "Aren't you going to have any breakfast?" She was whispering and trying not to stare the cat in the eyes. She knew he wouldn't like it.

Even though Helena didn't have
a cat, Gran had given her a book all
about them last Christmas. It was
because Helena had told Gran her
secret Christmas wish, when Gran
had asked what present she might
like. What Helena really wanted
for Christmas was a cat, but it was
a secret because Helena knew that

Mum would never let her have one.
She'd asked before, lots of times, and
Mum had always said no. Helena
could sort of see why – her mum was
a teacher at the school Helena went
to, so they were both out all day. A
kitten would be lonely and bored
and miserable, and Mum thought
it wasn't fair. Helena couldn't help
thinking that she could make the rest
of the time so special that the kitten
wouldn't mind. But she knew Mum
wouldn't agree.

Gran had given Helena a tiny china
cat and the book, which had loads of
beautiful photos and told you all the
things you needed to know to be a
cat owner. She'd written in the front
that Helena might not need it right

now, but she would have a cat of her own one day. And meanwhile, please could she come and practise on Gran's cats, Snow and Smudge, as they were getting fat and needed Helena to play with them!

On Saturday Helena had gone home and read everything she could find about cat injuries. After she'd read everything there was in the book from Gran, she'd gone online to look up more information. Now she was worried that the cat was traumatized by the accident. She'd had to get her mum to explain what traumatized meant. It was that the memory of the accident and the time at the vet's might make the cat really upset and perhaps not very friendly.

That made a lot of sense to Helena. She'd broken her arm falling off the climbing frame at school and even though that had been a year ago, she'd never gone back on the climbing frame.

Hopefully, if she made the little caramel cat's stay at the vet's as nice as possible, he'd think about that, rather than the car, and the cage, and his leg hurting. It had to be worth a try, Helena thought.

The cat sniffed at the food and even though cats didn't really shrug or sigh, Helena was almost sure he did. *I just can't be bothered*, he was thinking – she could tell.

He didn't even eat a mouthful.

Slowly, Helena reached into the cage and tickled him under the chin with one finger. He was such a handsome cat, even with the ugly plaster on his leg – a soft peachy colour all over, with darker caramel stripes and no white on him at all, apart from his drooping whiskers. His nose was apricot-pink and his eyes were huge and golden. He was going to be big, Helena thought, when he was fully grown. His paws were enormous, as though he needed to grow into them.

The cat curled himself into her hand a little, enjoying the soft touch of the girl's fingers. He didn't understand why he was here, shut up in this cage. The white thing was back on his leg

again and now it smelled even worse,
if that was possible. And it had tasted
disgusting when he'd tried chewing
at it. This whole place smelled wrong.
Too clean. He hated it. He wanted to
go back to his house and his garden,
and his little patch of street. But he
didn't know where home was – he
hadn't known for a while. He'd gone
exploring and then, somehow, he hadn't
known how to get back home. He
didn't understand it – he had thought
he would always know. But it had been
a long time now, and he'd been hungry
and tired and frightened when he tried
to cross that road. Now he was further
away from his home than ever.

He almost felt like whipping his
head round and nipping at the girl's

fingers with his teeth. But not quite. That patch under his chin was his favourite place to be stroked and she wasn't stopping. She'd reached all the itchy bits now and he wheezed out the faintest breath of a purr.

"Oh! Are you purring?" Helena whispered. "Are you feeling better?" She ran her hand gently over his smooth head and sighed. "If you don't have an owner, you'll have to go to the animal shelter when you're a bit better, so they can look after you till someone wants you. I hope you cheer up before then, caramel cat. You're so beautiful, and I think you'd be a lovely pet. But no one's going to take you home if you just hide at the back of your cage. You'll end up staying at the shelter for ages."

The little golden cat stayed flopped on his blanket and Helena tried not to think *Maybe for ever...*

Chapter Three

"So how's the cat now?" Helena's
friend Katie asked. "I suppose you
haven't seen him since yesterday."

"No, and I bet Mum's going to say
it's too late to nip over to the surgery on
the way home," Helena sighed. They
were waiting for Helena's mum to come
over from the staff room to pick them
up from football club after school.

She usually dropped Katie home too, or sometimes Katie stayed for tea. "She did let me text Lucy last night, and Lucy said he hadn't taken the cast off again. He still hadn't tried standing up, though, and he'd not eaten much."

"And nobody knows who he belongs to?" Katie asked anxiously. "Poor little cat! What's going to happen to him?"

Helena sighed. "Lucy said that if no one claims him in another day or so, he'll have to go to the shelter. But I don't think anyone's going to want a limpy, miserable cat who won't even come and say hello, even if he is pretty. They're putting a photo of him in the local paper too. Maybe his owner will see that."

"Sorry I'm late! Are you telling
Katie about the cat?" Helena's mum
had hurried up behind the girls
without them noticing. "I wonder if
they've found his owner yet."

"That's just what we were talking
about," Helena said, with a tiny sigh.
Of course, she did want the cat to go
back to his old home. But a little bit of
her was imagining him coming home
with her instead.

"Don't worry, Helena," her mum
said gently. "Even if he has to go to

the shelter, it'll be fine. I know quite a few people who've got their cats and dogs from there. The animals are looked after really well and the staff take a lot of care finding new homes for them."

"I suppose so," Helena murmured.

Katie gave her a sympathetic look – she realized what Helena was wishing. Her family had a fat black Labrador called Charlie and Helena loved to come with her to walk him. Katie knew how much her friend wanted a pet of her own.

Lucy called Helena that evening, while she was helping her mum make dinner.

"Has anyone phoned the surgery about the cat?" Helena asked her cousin hopefully. "Is he OK?"

"He's eating a bit better, but no, still no sign of an owner." There was a little silence, and then Lucy added, "I told Molly I'd take him home with me in a couple of days. Then I can try and find a home for him when he's better. I haven't broken it to Mum and Dad yet, though."

"Oh, that's brilliant!" Helena squealed, so loudly that her mum nearly dropped a pan of pasta. Lucy lived with her mum and dad, and her younger twin sisters, and their house wasn't far from Helena's. She'd still be able to see the cat all the time. She could go and visit him lots.

"I wasn't sure the staff at the shelter would have time to look after him properly. He needs a lot of TLC, poor thing."

"Definitely," Helena agreed. "Can I pop into the surgery with Gran after my dance lesson tomorrow? It'll be just as you're tidying everything up to go home. You know how much Gran loves cats. I told her about him."

Lucy giggled. "I'm just surprised she hasn't been round already. See you tomorrow then!"

"Here he is – he's a bit quiet still." Helena pointed out the caramel-coloured cat, huddled in the back of the cage and staring out at Helena's gran rather grumpily. But he shuffled towards the front of the cage when he saw Helena and she giggled. "That's right. You ought to be nice – I've brought you a present, look." She pulled a packet of cat treats out of her pocket and ripped the foil. "Tuna flavour! Mmmm... I think they smell awful, but the websites I looked at said most cats love the fishy ones."

"Beautiful colours in his fur…" Gran murmured. "So when are you taking him home, Lucy?"

"Tomorrow, I think." Lucy crouched down to look at the cat with them. "He really needs to get out of that little cage and start exercising his leg a bit more now it's beginning to heal. He's going to live in the utility room."

"What did your mum and dad say about it?" Helena asked.

Lucy made a face. "They weren't that keen… But I explained about the shelter being so busy and I promised we weren't keeping him for ever. Mum says I have to do all the washing, if there's to be a cat living in front of her washing machine…"

"Are you finishing work now, Lucy?"

300

Gran said, looking at her watch. "Do you want a lift home? I haven't seen Emily and Bella for at least a week. We could pop in and say hello."

Emily and Bella were Lucy's little sisters, Helena's cousins. They were only four. Helena loved going to see them – they were always so funny. Usually when she went round she got forced into having her hair redone in some mad style covered in feathers or glitter.

But as she sat in the back of Gran's car, she couldn't help thinking about the cat – so quiet and sad. How was he going to get on with two crazy four-year-olds? Not to mention Lucy's dog, Billy. He was about as silly as Emily and Bella, and he chased cats too.

Helena had
seen Lucy
hanging on to
the end of his
lead for dear
life when
they were out
for a walk and a cat strolled by.

Helena hugged Emily and Bella
when they jumped on her in the
hallway, and let them drag her upstairs
and paint her nails bright blue (Mum
would make her take it off again
before school, but never mind). But
she didn't enjoy her visit to her cousins'
house as much as she usually did.

She just couldn't imagine that
frightened little cat living here, even
for a short while. Billy was a lovely

dog (Emily and Bella had painted his nails blue too, and he'd let them) but Helena was sure that if he could smell a cat on the other side of the utility room door, he wouldn't rest until he'd clawed that door to shreds. It wasn't fair on Billy, either. And the caramel cat would be far too nervous to let Emily and Bella draw pictures all over his cast in sparkly pens.

It wasn't going to work.

"What's wrong, Helena?" Gran asked, as they got back into the car. "You've gone all quiet."

"The cat..." Helena said worriedly. "I'm not sure he'll be able to cope with

Lucy's house, Gran. I'm not being mean – it's just he's still so nervous and there's so much going on there. I think it'll make him worse."

Gran sighed. "I was wondering about that too. But Lucy said he'll be shut away in one room…"

"Yeah, but there's no way Emily and Bella will leave him in there," Helena pointed out. "They'll be dressing him in their dolls' clothes the minute Auntie Sam's back is turned."

"Mmmm." Gran drove down the road, frowning to herself. "I wish I could take him…"

"Snow and Smudge wouldn't like it, though, would they?" Helena sighed. "Everyone's already got cats, or dogs, or twins." She was silent for a minute, and then added, "Except us. Me and Mum. Mum's always said no, because it wouldn't be good for a cat to be left alone, but this cat needs to have some peace and quiet. Don't you think so, Gran?"

"And I could always pop in and see him at lunch time. Make a little fuss over him." Gran darted a hopeful glance at Helena. "You know, maybe we could persuade your mum together."

"She already said he was gorgeous when Lucy showed her the photo on her phone." Helena wound her hands together, over and over. She was suddenly so excited she couldn't keep still.

If only they could convince her mum…

Chapter Four

"But we can't... We don't have anywhere to keep him."

"We do, Mum! In here – in the kitchen would be all right. He couldn't jump on the counter. We could put a blanket in that space under the counter for him, with his food bowls and litter tray, and I promise I'd clean it out, always."

"I can come and check on him, Clare, at lunch time," Gran suggested.

Helena's mum frowned, looking round at her little kitchen.

"He can't go to Lucy's house, Mum," said Helena. "And he'll be miserable at the shelter, I know he will. No one's come to claim him, even though we put posters up all round where we found him and in the vet's window. He's been in the local paper today, with a message saying to ring the surgery, but no one has yet. Maybe his owner will see the photo, but he was so thin, Lucy thinks that could mean he's been a stray for a while. I want to be able to look after him. It feels like I have to, since I was the one who found him."

Her mum was silent for a moment, then she turned round to look at her. "I suppose not. Oh, Helena. It's going to be a lot of work, you know. But I am proud of you."

"You mean ... yes?" Helena asked, confused. She'd expected to have to beg for an awful lot longer than that. And even then, deep down, she'd been almost certain that her mum would never agree.

"Yes. I mean, we'd have to give him back, if his real owner contacted the surgery, but yes. Do you think he could stay at the vet's until the weekend?" her mum asked. "Then we'd have two whole days to get him used to being at our house, before we have to leave him on his own."

The cat was sitting up the next afternoon when Helena brought her mum to meet him. He peered out of the cage bars, waiting for her. He could hear her talking to someone in the next room, and she sounded excited and happy. She had brought him cat treats the last time she came, fishy ones that he liked. And sometimes she opened the front of the cage and sat for ages, stroking his fur and murmuring to him. She made him feel safe. Even when he was stuck here in this place that wasn't his home and he could smell the dogs at the other end of the room.

He sat up, wondering if perhaps she'd let him out of the cage this time. He could sit on her, and then she'd be able to stroke him better and rub his ears.

When he saw the girl come in, he skittered nervously back, knocking his cast against the floor of the cage.

She wasn't on her own – the young woman was with her, the one he saw every day, and someone else too.

"It's all right," Helena murmured. "This is my mum. We'll be taking you home to our house soon…"

The caramel cat didn't know what Helena was saying but he liked hearing her soft voice. And the other person spoke softly too.

"He's beautiful, Helena. Even more than in the photos. What are we going to call him? Or have you named him already?"

Helena opened the door of the cage and the cat stepped out slowly, sniffing at her outstretched hand. She rubbed the dark caramel stripes between his ears and smiled at her mum.

"I haven't really named him. But when I think about him, I call him the cat with the caramel fur. Do you think we could call him Caramel?"

"We're here!" Helena said gratefully, turning round to peer at the crate strapped into the back seat. Caramel had been howling dismally ever since Mum drove off. He clearly hated the crate and didn't like the feeling of the moving car at all.

"Do you think being in a car reminds him of the accident?" she asked her mum worriedly.

"No – I think all cats hate being in boxes. Shut in them, I mean. They like getting in by themselves." Her mum turned off the engine and looked round too. "Even when he's been in the cage at the vet's for a whole week, it's not the same. He can't see out of that travelling basket very well. He'll be much better when we let him into the kitchen."

"It'll probably feel huge," Helena agreed, opening her door and going to get the basket out of the back. "We're here, Caramel. This is your house now too. Just your kitchen for the minute, though. But Molly says you'll be able to have the plaster off in about three more weeks, since you're still a kitten and you'll heal quicker than a big cat." She carried the box into the house as she chatted to him and her mum came in behind her, shutting the door of their little kitchen. There were only the worktops in there, and the oven and the fridge, and Helena was almost sure Caramel wouldn't be able to jump up on those. So it was a safe place to keep him.

"Look," she said gently, unlatching the top of the box and taking it off, so Caramel could decide to come out when he wanted to. "There's a special soft basket for you. And a litter tray.

And I'll get you some food."

They had gone to the pet shop the night before and got it all – the travel box, the cushiony basket and the food bowls. It had been so exciting. Helena had looked at cat toys as well, but they hadn't bought any, not for the moment. They were all designed for chasing and rolling and batting with paws, and Caramel needed to stay quiet and rest. Helena promised herself she'd go back, once he was better.

Caramel sat pressed against the back of the crate, looking around suspiciously. He hadn't understood what was happening when they'd lifted him out of the cage and into this horrible little box. Then he'd thought that perhaps they were going home. It had been such a long time since he'd been there.

He hunched his shoulders, ears laid back, and watched Helena and her mum both watching him. But they were quiet and still, and no one was grabbing at him. The fur along his spine flattened down a little and he padded his paws thoughtfully into the blanket. Then he sniffed and shook his ears, standing up a bit lopsided. This wasn't his old house, of course. But it smelled good. Not like the surgery, full of sharp strong smells that hurt his nose. This place smelled of the girl and food. He lurched out of the basket, his plastered leg tangling in the blanket, and set out to explore.

"I thought he was never going to come out," Helena breathed to her mum, watching Caramel sniff the doors of the cupboards.

"I know. Why don't you put some food down for him?"

Helena stood up. She tried to do it very carefully and slowly, but Caramel still flinched back against the cupboards when he saw her move. It made her want to cry. "It's all right. I was just getting you some breakfast," she murmured. "Lucy said she didn't feed you this morning, just in case you were sick in your basket."

She fetched one of the tins out of the cupboard and pulled up the ring on the lid. Then she laughed as Caramel hurried across the kitchen floor, his plastered leg knocking on the tiles. "You sound like a pirate cat, with a wooden leg," she told him, as she put the bowl down.

"I'm so glad he's eating," her mum said, leaning against the counter to watch him.

"I know – I was worried he'd be too upset being in a new place," Helena agreed. "But look at him, he's wolfing that down." She stood up, putting an arm round her mum. "Thanks for letting us have him."

"You're not disappointed?" Mum asked. "I mean – it's not like having a normal cat. He's not very friendly. And he can't sleep on your bed or anything like that."

Helena shrugged. "I know. But he will be able to one day. And I know he's not that friendly yet, but think how special it will be when he *is*."

She crouched down again to watch

Caramel licking out his food bowl. He'd definitely got his appetite back, and he was making sure to get every last morsel of food. He stood up again, rather clumsily, and licked his whiskers.

Chapter Five

Caramel uncurled himself from his basket as he heard footsteps coming towards the kitchen door. The girl. And probably breakfast. He hobbled to the door to meet her, rubbing hopefully round her ankles. She crouched down to stroke him – but he noticed she carefully shut the kitchen door first, so he couldn't dart round it. She murmured to him as she scratched the satin-soft puffs of fur at the base of his ears and he leaned against her lovingly.

Helena had spent a lot of the weekend sitting next to him on the floor, letting him get used to her being around. She'd even done her homework sitting on the kitchen floor. When Caramel had tried to steal her pencil while she was doing long division, it had been one of the best moments of the weekend. It proved he was happy enough to play.

"I wish I didn't have to go to school today…" Helena told him, as she scooped food into his bowl. "Urgh, this smells disgusting, Caramel. I don't know how you can be so excited about it." She giggled, watching him waltz

around her feet, waiting
for her to put the bowl
down. He still didn't
like moving his broken
leg much, so that leg
stayed still and the rest
of him whirled around,
a bit like a spinning top.

He started to gobble the
food before she'd even put the bowl
down, stretching up to get his mouth
over the edge of the bowl and patting
at it with one golden paw.

"You're definitely getting better,"
Helena said, watching happily as
he gulped the food down. "Are you
making up for all those days at the
vet's when you didn't eat properly?
I do still wonder if you were a stray

for a while before the accident. You're ever so thin. And otherwise I'm sure your owners would have seen our posters if they lived anywhere near. We put them everywhere."

Caramel was just finishing the food when Helena's mum hurried into the kitchen. She was a bit late getting breakfast ready and she was rushing. She banged the door open without thinking and Caramel shot into the corner, trembling and pressing himself against the side of the cupboard.

"Mum! You scared him!" Helena gasped.

"Oh! Sorry, Caramel…" Her mum shut the door gently and crouched down, holding her hand out for the frightened cat to sniff. "I'm really sorry, Helena, I didn't realize the door would frighten him so much. He's been so good this weekend."

"I know…" Helena agreed sadly. "But I suppose he's still upset, deep down. It's going to take a while for him to get over that." She looked at her mum. "He will be happier again one day, won't he?"

"I'm sure he will."

But Helena didn't think her mum was very sure at all.

"Be good, Caramel." Helena ran her hand lovingly down his silky back. "Have lots of lovely sleep. Gran's going to come and see you at lunch time and

I bet she'll bring you treats."

Caramel stood in the middle of the kitchen, looking up at her uncertainly. He wasn't sure what was happening. Since he had arrived at Helena's house, early on Saturday morning, Helena had been with him almost all the time. She had even come down in the middle of the night to check on him. But now she had a coat on and a bag with her. It looked as though she was leaving him behind.

At his old house, his owner had gone out to work most days. Caramel had lazed the time away, curled up on the back of the sofa so that he could watch the people passing in the street. And the cars. Caramel laid his ears back with a frightened little hiss.

Most days he'd slipped out of his cat flap and patrolled his territory in the gardens behind the house. There were several other cats in the street, and he was one of the youngest and newest, so he'd had to be careful to stay out of their way. But he still had plenty to explore. There was a pond a few houses away and he liked to watch the frogs. And catch them, sometimes. He could creep up on them among the plants around the water. But his owner hadn't liked it when

Caramel had brought one home. He had taken Caramel's frog outside and locked the cat flap so that he couldn't slip out and fetch it back in again.

But here, there was no window to watch from and no cat flap to slide out of. He was all alone in this little room. It was better than the cage at the vet's surgery, of course, but being shut up still made him want to claw at the door and fight his way out. When would Helena and her mother come back? Perhaps they weren't coming back at all? His old owner had fussed over him, and fed him, and loved him, but now he was gone. Maybe Helena had gone too. Caramel stared anxiously at the kitchen door, hoping to hear them coming back. But there wasn't a sound.

Perhaps he could go and find them himself?

Caramel hobbled across the tiled floor, sniffing hopefully at the door out to the garden. There was a faint breath of fresh air around the side of the door – just enough to make him desperate to go out. He scratched at the door but not very hard. He could already see that he wasn't going to be able to get out.

Wearily, he trailed back to his basket. His broken back leg was aching, not used to carrying his weight. Caramel snuggled into the basket and hoped that Helena hadn't left him for ever. He hoped that she would come back soon.

Chapter Six

"So does anyone have any exciting news from their weekend?" Miss Smith looked round at the class as she finished marking the register.

"Tell her!" Katie hissed, nudging Helena in the ribs with her elbow. "Helena does, Miss Smith!"

Helena went pink but she nodded. "I've got a cat."

"Oh, lovely!" Miss Smith smiled. "Where did you get him from, Helena? Or her?"

"He's a he. And he came from the vet's where my cousin Lucy works," Helena explained. "He was run over last weekend."

Everyone in the class sat up and started listening more closely. Until then there'd been a bit of a Monday-ish feeling going on, and most people had been staring vaguely at the whiteboard, or whispering to each other.

"Run over?" one of the boys asked. "What happened, was he hurt?"

Helena nodded. "He's got a fractured back leg. But he was lucky. Often they have to operate on cats and put pins in, but he's just got a cast."

331

"But who does he belong to?" Miss Smith asked, sounding a little confused. "Was he a stray? Has no one claimed him?"

"No. And the vet's even put a little article about him in the local paper. That page where the animal shelter usually puts a photo of a cat or dog that needs a home."

"Oh, that's how we got our dog!" Marley called out. "We saw him in the paper."

"Mm-hm. The article was in on Wednesday. But still no one claimed him. So we reckoned it was OK to take him home. We think maybe he's been lost for a while, even before he got hit by the car. He's quite thin."

"Show them the photo," Katie

suggested, and Helena pulled it out of her bag. She'd brought it in to show Katie and a couple of her other friends. It was Caramel curled up asleep in his basket, and you could see his plaster cast. She passed it round, and all the class murmured about how cute he was and how sad his leg looked.

"He's come home with us because otherwise he would have had to go to the animal shelter," Helena went on. "He's been really lucky. All his vet care's been paid for by donations from the shelter he almost went to and the PDSA."

"The what?" someone called.

"It's a charity, isn't it?" Miss Smith asked.

Helena nodded. "It stands for People's Dispensary for Sick Animals. It's a big charity, but they have a clinic close to here, in Thirtover Road. They look after animals when people can't afford to pay. Vet bills can be really, really expensive. Thousands of pounds, my cousin told me."

Helena frowned thoughtfully. Ever since Molly had told her that the PDSA were helping to pay back the surgery for Caramel's treatment, she'd been wishing she could do something to help. Something more than just giving them her pocket money. She'd already decided to get her mum to buy their Christmas cards from the PDSA – they made very cute ones with cats and dogs in the snow – but it would be good to think of a way to raise some money too. So that if another cat got hurt like Caramel, there wouldn't be a worry about having enough money to look after it.

Lucy had said that when she'd phoned the shelter to tell them that they wouldn't have to take Caramel after all, the girl on the phone had been relieved. She'd said they were full to bursting. They needed a lot of money just to feed all the animals, let alone pay for vet care.

"Miss Smith, do you think we could try to make some money for the PDSA and some for the shelter? We could have a cake sale or something?" Helena asked hopefully. "Mr Brown said he wanted all the junior classes to think about fundraising for charities. It was in assembly, back at the beginning of term."

"He did…" Miss Smith agreed. "It's a good idea. What about the rest of the class, though? What do you all think?"

"I definitely want to raise some money for the shelter!" Marley nodded. "There were loads of other dogs there when we went to get Chester. It was really sad – my mum cried. And the other charity sounds good too," he added.

Everyone in the class was nodding, but Alice, another of Helena's friends, waved her hand at Miss Smith. "Can we do something different, though?

Everyone does cake sales."

"That's because everyone likes cake!" Katie pointed out, and Alice shrugged.

"It's still a bit boring."

"So what do you want to do instead?" Miss Smith grinned. "How about a sponsored silence?"

Lots of people groaned and Helena twisted her fingers in her hair, trying to think. They needed to come up with a good idea and quickly, before people lost interest. Already a couple of the boys were suggesting a sponsored parachute jump. It would just get silly in a minute. She put her hand up, looking hopefully at Miss Smith.

"We ought to do something that's about pets. Since that's what we're raising money for."

"Like a dog show!" Alice suggested, but Miss Smith looked rather horrified.

"Sorry, I don't think Mr Brown would let us have a dog show in school," she said firmly.

"But we could have a sort of competition," Helena said slowly. "With videos of our pets, instead of bringing the actual pets in! Like a funniest pet competition. We could ask the whole school if they wanted to enter. And the teachers! Mr Brown's got a really cute dog, hasn't he?"

"I could borrow my mum's phone and film Charlie skateboarding," Katie yelped excitedly. "He's not very good at it but he loves trying. It's really funny to watch."

"And people could pay a little bit to enter," Helena said, still trying to think it through. "Then we could show all the videos one lunch time. And sell tickets – oh, and have cakes and biscuits for sale too," she added to Katie.

"I'll ask Mr Brown about it at break," Miss Smith said, as the whole class tried to tell her about their pets' funniest tricks at once. "And then maybe we can use your IT lesson this afternoon to make some posters."

Helena hopped impatiently from foot to foot as her mum unlocked the front door. Gran had sent Mum a text saying that Caramel had been fine at lunch time. But Helena was desperate to see for herself that he was all right. She rushed in as soon as Mum got the door open, making for the kitchen.

"Oh! Listen!" she told her mum, stopping in the hall. "He's mewing... And I can hear him – he's got out of his basket, he's coming to see us!" There was definitely a thumping noise coming from behind the kitchen door, as Caramel limped determinedly towards them. Helena giggled. "Maybe I can film you doing your pirate walk for our competition," she told Caramel, as she carefully opened the kitchen door. "Whoa! No dashing out..." She caught him gently. "Sorry, Caramel-cat. You have to stay in here."

Caramel half climbed into her lap and rubbed his chin against her school jumper.

"Is he purring?" Mum whispered.

Helena looked up at her and nodded. She actually hadn't dared to say anything. It was only the second time she'd heard him purr. And that first time at the vet's he had only purred for a second or two, very faintly. Now Caramel was purring properly. A deep throaty purr that Helena could feel as well as hear. He was quivering all over with purrs.

"He's glad to see us," she whispered to Mum. "He's actually happy!"

Chapter Seven

"He's definitely looking better," Katie said after school the next day, watching Caramel trying to investigate the fridge. Helena had opened it to get out the butter and Caramel could smell the ham for her packed lunches. It smelled delicious – and very close to his nose.

"He is, isn't he," Helena agreed happily. "No, you can't climb in there!"

She nudged Caramel back with her toe and closed the door. "Sorry. Am I mean, puss?"

Caramel stalked away with his tail in the air, as though he wasn't bothered, but his plastered leg made it a bit tricky. He was still feeling wobbly.

"He looked quite sad in that photo you brought in," Katie said. "But now he's cheered up a lot, I think. It's lovely to finally meet him in person. Caramel! Puss, puss, puss…" She made kissy noises and Caramel padded cautiously across the floor towards her, sniffing her outstretched fingers, and letting her rub his head and tickle his ears.

"He's much more friendly now," Helena said happily. "I don't think he'd have done that on Saturday when we brought him home. When you think that it's only Wednesday, he's got ever so much better and in such a short time. When he was still at the vet's he was so shy and miserable. He's quite nervous sometimes, though," she added. "He hates loud noises."

"He walks really well, doesn't he," Katie said, watching Caramel prowl round their ankles as they weighed out the ingredients for their biscuits.

"He's putting weight on his bad leg a bit more now. Before he was sort of hopping, as if he was trying not to put it down to the ground. He's got another two and a half weeks and then hopefully he can have the plaster taken off. Oh, please can you pass me the sugar?"

The two girls were making cat-shaped biscuits to sell at the Funniest Pet Show. Mr Brown, the head teacher, had said it was a great idea, very creative. He'd told them to go ahead and arrange the show for Friday when he'd be able to judge.

"Did you send in a video of Caramel with his plaster on?" Katie asked. "I've done Charlie – he was brilliant. The skateboard went out from under his paws and he just sort of stared at it as if he didn't understand what had happened."

"Yes, I sent it, but I don't think he'll win," Katie said, shaking her head. "Some of the others are so funny. Bella's cat trying to drink out of the

taps in the washbasin is the best,
I reckon. It's the way she turns her
head upside down and then shakes all
the water off her whiskers. It makes
me laugh every time."

Helena and some of the others in her
class had been watching all the videos
with their teacher during break and
lunch to find the best ones that would
be in the show – they'd meant to put
them all in, but there were so many,
there wasn't time to let everyone watch
them all. They had already made more
than eighty pounds, just from people
paying a pound to send in a video.
Then they were selling tickets for the
show, and everyone in the class was
supposed to be bringing some cakes or
biscuits in to sell too.

"We should have got orangey-gold icing for the eyes on these biscuits," Katie said, peering down at Caramel, who'd gone to sit in his basket under the counter, since they clearly weren't going to feed him anything. "I hadn't noticed before what a lovely colour his eyes are."

"I know," Helena agreed proudly. "Mum and I talked about doing the eyes gold when we made the shopping list, but we decided green ones were more usual. Caramel's just extra-specially beautiful."

"He looks like he's sulking," Katie said. "Is he OK? He's got his nose tucked away inside his basket."

Helena looked down under the counter and sighed. "I think that now he's walking better, it's making him cross being shut in the kitchen. Every time we open the kitchen door, he's there, trying to slip round our legs. He never scratches or bites, but you can tell he's annoyed. His ears go all flat and his tail's twitchy. He wants to go and explore."

"Couldn't you let him out?" Katie asked. "Why does he have to stay in the kitchen?"

"Molly – that's the vet – she said that if he tried to climb or jump he could jar his broken leg and stop it healing. Even if it was just trying to climb the stairs, he might trip and fall because of the plaster. There's nowhere in the kitchen that he can reach to jump up to, but there's enough space for him to exercise his leg muscles. Otherwise his leg's going to go all thin and weak inside the plaster."

"Oh, I see." Katie nodded. "That's sensible."

"Mmmm, Caramel doesn't think so, though. He thinks we're just being mean." Helena sighed. "Little grumpy-face," she told Caramel lovingly.

Caramel heard her and looked up. He gazed at her for a moment and then yawned hugely, showing all his teeth and his bright pink tongue.

Helena giggled. "See? That's what he thinks of us..."

Caramel sat by the back door, his nose pressed against the narrow crack between the door and the frame. There was something out in the garden, he was sure. He could hear it – a bird, perhaps, tapping and twittering around on the little stone patio. He ached to be out there too, smelling the smells, chasing the birds. Just feeling the air ruffling up his fur. He hated being an inside cat.

He paced up and down beside the door for a few moments, letting out a frustrated mew. His leg was so much better now. It felt stronger. He was sure he could even climb a tree, if only they would let him out. Or maybe scramble up on to the top of a fence, just to get a good look around. He wanted to see what the outside was like round here. He was so sick of being shut up indoors.

His ears twitched as he caught a sound from the front of the house – footsteps on the path, and now scratching as someone fiddled with the front door. Helena was back!

No. His shoulders sagged a little. It wasn't the right time. It would be that other lady come to check on him.

"Hello, Caramel…" Gran was squeezing carefully round the door, making sure not to let him dart out. "How are you, darling? Want some of these nice little biscuit things?" She brought a packet out of her handbag, and Caramel sniffed as she pulled it open and the delicious smell wafted around. But somehow, it just wasn't very exciting. Not nearly as good as the fresh air smell through the back door. It was starting to rain now. He could smell the wet pavement smell and hear the heavy fat drops pattering down on the stone. He wanted to be out in it. Not for long – just enough to feel the freshness, and then dash back in and lick off all the water. It would be so good...

"Oh, it's raining! And I didn't bring an umbrella – what a nuisance." Gran was staring out of the window, looking irritated. "And look, Caramel, they've got washing out! Well, that's going to get soaked. And there's Helena's school jumper. I wonder if she needs that for tomorrow... Drat it, I'll have to go and bring it all in."

She put down her bag on the counter and hurried to the door, jingling the keys as she unlocked it.

Caramel hadn't understood what

she was saying about the washing, of course, but he knew what the sound of the keys meant. She was letting him out! He stood by her feet, his tail twitching excitedly and his whiskers fanned and bristling. Out! After all this time! As the door opened, he darted round Gran's feet, his caramel fur brushing against her legs, and hopped down the little step on to the patio.

Gran was thinking about the washing, not about Caramel, and so she didn't realize what had happened until it was too late. "Oh! Oh, no! You're not supposed to go out! Oh, my goodness, how stupid of me..." She abandoned the washing and went after the cat. "Caramel! Come on... Caramel... Puss, puss..."

But Caramel was
sniffing at
the flower
pots and
twitching
delightedly
at the feel of
the rain on his fur. He could smell
other cats, which was interesting and
dangerous and exciting. And perhaps
a dog, close by, and there was a beetle
walking along in front of his nose...
Everything was good...

"Come here, Caramel, come on,
you'll hurt yourself..." Gran reached
down and tried to grab him, but
Caramel skittered out of reach, his
cast knocking on the stone paving and
throwing him off balance.

He hissed as a twinge of pain ran through his injured leg, and backed away furiously.

"Oh no…" Gran hurried after him, but Caramel hissed again, frightened and hurting, and darted away around the corner of the house, up the little side passage where the bins were.

Gran was chasing him but he didn't want to be caught. His leg was throbbing as he scurried up the passage and now there was a gate, shutting him in again. Caramel spat angrily and pressed up against it. He wasn't going to let her grab him! He couldn't be shut up inside again. He darted a clawed paw at Gran as she came close and reached to pick him up. Desperate, he squashed himself down and scrabbled under the wooden boards, dragging his plastered leg behind him. He struggled, mewing, for a second – and then he was out, at the front of the house, on the road.

Once he'd squeezed under the gate, Caramel hobbled out on to the pavement, going as fast as he could with his plastered leg. He was determined not to let Gran catch him. He scurried along the pavement and darted behind someone's wheelie bin when he heard the gate squeak open, and Gran dash out after him. He could hear her calling but he stayed tucked behind the bin.

Caramel peered out, watching
her, and when she hurried off the
other way down the road, he pressed
himself close against the garden wall
and slunk away. Everything smelled
so good in the damp, rain-fresh air.
His leg was aching a little – he hadn't
gone so fast or so far on it for ages –
but he didn't mind. He was so tired of
cages and that tiny room.

The rain had stopped now and the clouds were blowing over. He shivered with pleasure as he felt the warm autumn sun shining down on his fur. That was what he wanted to do! He would find somewhere to lie in the sun. If only Gran hadn't been chasing him, he could have stayed in the little garden at the back of Helena's house. He was sure there would have been a nice sunny place to curl up. And when Helena came home, she could stroke him while he snoozed.

He glanced uncertainly back down the road. He could go and see. He could squeeze back under the gate… But he could hear Gran calling him, her voice more and more worried. That high, panicked note made the fur lift a little along his spine and he hurried on a few steps further.

He couldn't go too far, though, he realized, after he'd gone past a few more houses. It was hard, half hopping along with his cast like this, and he was already getting tired.

He was looking around, wondering where he could go and rest and sleep in the sun for a little while, when he heard it. It drowned out Gran's shouting – the low rumble of a car, heading down the road towards him.

Caramel's ears went back and his tail fluffed out to twice its normal size. He had heard cars before, of course. But now the sound reminded him of the accident and that strange blaze of light, and then waking up to find he couldn't walk.

He whipped his head desperately
from side to side as the growl of the
car grew louder, and as it roared
past he shot into the nearest garden,
forgetting how much his leg was
hurting and how weary he was. He
had to get away.

Caramel darted under the bushes,
not even noticing how wet they were.
And then he huddled there, shivering
and terrified, and wishing he'd never
strayed outside the house.

Chapter Eight

"You let him out?" Helena gaped at Gran as they stood outside the gates after school. She couldn't understand it. For a moment when Gran had started to explain, Helena had thought that she must be joking – that it was some sort of silly story, but it wasn't.

"I'm so sorry, Helena, I wasn't thinking. It was the washing, you see

– I had to get it in because of the rain. Oh, I'm not explaining this very well."

Gran looked exhausted, Helena realized. She'd probably spent ages getting Caramel back in. She felt guilty for being angry, but only a little bit. How could Gran have let him out, when it was so important that he stayed in the kitchen?

"He slipped past me. He was so quick…"

"We might need to get him to the vet's to see if he's damaged his leg." Helena started off down the road towards home, weaving round everyone pouring out of the school gates. Usually they went back to Gran's house on the days that Mum was working late, but Helena was sure Gran would understand that she wanted to check up on Caramel first.

"How did you get him back in?" she asked, turning to look at Gran, who was hurrying after her.

Gran stopped and simply stared at her, and Helena's stomach seemed to lurch inside her. All at once, she knew what Gran had been trying to make her understand.

She hadn't got him back. Caramel was lost!

Helena turned back, looking at the road and the cars flashing by, taking everyone home from school. Then she simply ran. She ran all the way home, ignoring Gran calling after her. After a little while, she couldn't hear Gran shouting anyway.

Her mouth was dry, her heart racing. She was so horribly certain that as she turned into their street, she would see the little heap of sandy fur again. And that this time, Caramel wouldn't have been so lucky. He had his leg in plaster – how could he get out of the way of a car?

When she turned the corner into their road, Helena stopped for a moment, panting, her face scarlet. There was no cat in the road, not that she could see. And no crowd of horrified passers-by. She took a deep, shuddering breath and went on, hurrying up their side of the road, and then carefully crossing over and checking the other side. Looking under all the cars.

At last she stopped, leaning against the front wall of their house and trying not to cry. Where was he? Gran had tried to explain that he'd run under the side gate, so he must have come out on to the road. Perhaps he was just hiding somewhere, Helena thought, with a sudden jolt of hope. She dropped her school bag by the front door and set off up the road, calling. "Caramel! Caramel!"

But he didn't come and she couldn't even hear an answering mew. She flinched as a car sped past, wanting to shout after the driver to slow down. What if Caramel ran across the road to get to her?

Would he come anyway? Helena wondered worriedly. Perhaps he didn't know her well enough to want to come back. He'd only lived with them for half a week, after all. But he'd been getting so friendly – she had really felt like he was their cat.

Perhaps he'd gone back to his old house – his old owner – if he knew where it was. Helena gulped back tears.

"Helena!" Gran was hurrying down the road towards her. "Oh, I was so worried. You crossed all those roads on your own."

Helena stared back at her. "I'm sorry, Gran," she said breathlessly. She'd been so frightened, she'd just thought about getting home and finding Caramel, nothing else.

"He's not here, Gran…" Helena said miserably. "I've called and called. Maybe he's gone back to his old home. Or he might just be lost. He might be one of those cats who doesn't have a good sense of direction. He'll never find his way back to us!"

Gran wrapped her arms round Helena. "We must be able to find him," she murmured. "I'm so sorry, Helena. Surely he can't be far away."

Caramel
could hear
Helena
calling him
and his ears pricked
forwards hopefully. She sounded
worried, but he knew her far better
than Gran and he was sure she wasn't
angry. He stirred under the bushes,
trying to summon up the energy to
get back on to his aching leg and
go to her. But as he poked his nose
out from under the plants, another
car came racing by and he pressed
himself back into the leaves with a
frightened hiss.

He couldn't move. He just couldn't.
Even though he could hear Helena
calling him again and again, and her

gran and later her mum too, he was too frightened to come out. Every few minutes a car would go by and Caramel froze, paralysed by the noise.

He wriggled back even further when a car pulled up outside the house and footsteps echoed beside his hiding place. It was getting dark and cold. The cold made his injured leg ache even more and he shivered miserably. The lights came on in the house behind him and that just made the night seem darker. He wanted to be home, with Helena putting down his food bowl and watching him eat.

There were fewer cars now, though, he realized. He had been hiding there for hours, waiting for the next one to

roar past, his muscles tensed in case
it came close. He edged out from
the bushes, his whiskers twitching
nervously as he sniffed the night air.
Helena's house was only a little way
down the road. He knew it.

He could get home, if only he
were brave enough to come out of his
hiding place.

And it *was* home, he realized.
He wanted to be back with Helena.
Even if they did keep him shut up.
The house was safe and warm, and
they would look after him. Caramel
limped out of the tiny front garden
and crouched by the wall, his ears laid
back. No cars. It was time to go.

Helena was sitting curled up in bed, in the dark. She'd tried to sleep – Mum kept coming in and checking on her, and last time Helena had actually pretended she was asleep. She didn't want Mum to tell her all over again that it would be all right and they'd probably find Caramel tomorrow. Mum didn't know that! She was just saying it to make her feel better. And it wasn't working.

Helena sniffed. She had tried so hard to look after Caramel, but it would have been better if he'd gone to the shelter after all. He wouldn't have been able to run away there and he'd still be safe. She felt a choking feeling build up in her throat again and she tried desperately to swallow it back down.

What if they never saw him again?

Helena gulped and buried her nose in her duvet, trying to muffle the gasping, horrible noises she was making. It was really late – Mum was probably asleep. She sat there, curled up and shaking, tears making a great wet patch on her duvet.

He hadn't been hit by another car, Helena tried to tell herself. They had searched all the streets nearby and they hadn't found him. And Gran had rung Lucy to check he hadn't been brought into the surgery. He was just hiding somewhere. She pressed her face back into the duvet, thinking how cold and frightened Caramel must be. The wind lashed raindrops against her window again – it was such a horrible night to be outside.

Then another sound made Helena look up. She could hardly hear it, with the wind blowing, and at first she'd thought it was just the rain. But it wasn't – she knew that noise! That odd knocking, like a pirate walking on his wooden leg. Helena wriggled frantically, trying to unwind herself from her duvet. It was Caramel!

She jumped out of bed, racing to the

window. She could hear him mewing now too. She wrenched open her curtains and shoved the window open, leaning down to see into the garden.

And he was there! A small, bedraggled, golden cat, yowling at her in the moonlight. He'd come home!

"Look, Caramel," Helena told him proudly, as she stuck the certificate on to the fridge door with a magnet. "Bella's cat won the prize for the most amazing pet! I told you she would, but you were second! And do you know how much money we raised altogether? Three hundred pounds! That's a lot," she added, as Caramel rubbed himself around her knees. "Yes, I know. You don't care at all, you just want me to get the cat food out. All right."

She looked down at him as she squeezed the food into his bowl. His fur was soft and caramelly again, and he was only limping a little. Last night, when she'd run downstairs, and out into the garden to scoop him up, his coat had been dark and spiky with rain, and he'd looked so miserable. His leg had obviously been hurting too. She and Mum had dried him with a towel and he'd purred at them gratefully. Helena had been worried that the rain had softened the cast, or that he'd made the break worse, but Molly had driven round and looked at him, and said that luckily it was all right. She thought Caramel was just limping because he'd been putting more weight on his leg than he was used to.

"Only another two weeks," Helena told Caramel, as she kneeled on the floor, watching him licking out his bowl. "Molly said she was almost sure the cast could come off after that. Then you'll be able to explore the rest of the house. And go outside."

Caramel sniffed round the edge of the bowl, just in case any food had escaped, and then nosed lovingly at Helena's hand. He yawned and licked his whiskers, then climbed determinedly into her lap. He flopped down, stretching his plastered leg sideways and kneaded at her school skirt with his front paws. He was glad to be home.

Helena giggled and shifted her feet a little, so she wouldn't get pins and needles. It looked like Caramel was staying for a while.

Out Now

From MULTI-MILLION best-selling author

Holly Webb

The
**Puppy Who
Ran Away**

Illustrated by Sophy Williams

Out Now

From MULTI-MILLION best-selling author

Holly Webb

Nadia and the Forever Kitten

Illustrated by Sophy Williams

HOLLY WEBB

Holly Webb started out as a children's book editor and wrote her first series for the publisher she worked for. She has been writing ever since, with over one hundred books to her name. Holly lives in Berkshire, with her husband and three children. Holly's pet cats are always nosying around when she is trying to type on her laptop.

For more information
about Holly Webb visit:

www.holly-webb.com